Siren's Blood

WILD MAGIC: SIREN'S SECRET
BOOK ONE

STEPHANIE MIRRO

Linley Press

Siren's Gift

Siren's Legacy

COLLECTIONS

The Outsiders: An Hourlings Anthology

I love to get to know my readers. Find me on Facebook, Instagram, or Twitter **@stephaniemirro**.

Visit stephaniemirro.com for more information on each of my books.

For Merpeople the world over,

I sea you, and I love you. Thank you for inspiring me when I needed it the most.

"A mermaid has not an immortal soul, nor can she obtain one unless she wins the love of a human being." - Hans Christian Anderson

CHAPTER 1

Bree

I wanted to punch a baby. I mean, not literally, because that was just cruel and unusual and, frankly, psychotic. But my little sister knew exactly how to take me from feeling like a serene, undisturbed lake to a raging hurricane hellbent on utter destruction in two seconds flat.

It was a gift, really.

"What do you mean you'll lose your scholarship if I don't help you?" I ground out into my wireless earbuds. Beads of sweat trickled down my back, a lovely reminder of the task I needed to complete.

Marissa always had the best timing.

Why had I agreed to get a cell phone again?

I tightened my grip on the mop's handle. Oh right, because I had a sister determined to send me to an early grave.

"Wait, what took you so long to answer?" Her voice was hoarse, which didn't bode well for where this conversation was headed. "Toilets clogged again?"

"No, Benson wasn't here last night, thank the tides." I

shuddered, fighting to keep those stomach-churning memories from rising. I'd almost quit that day.

Some people might think the worst part of my job was cleaning up blood, but it wasn't. Not by a long shot. You see, the blood that was spilled and flung across the fighting ring and surrounding crowd wasn't due to disrespect or not giving a hoot. Quite the opposite.

The fighters gave life and honor to the ring by spilling their blood.

So what was the worst part?

Cleaning the bathrooms after a fight night.

Good gods, men had *zero* aim after getting hit in the head or squinting between blackened and swollen eyelids. To be fair, most had poor aim no matter the circumstance, but everything was worse if they got punched in their gut or had anxiety shits. *Way* worse.

Women weren't much better either.

Nausea churned in my stomach again. I needed to stop thinking about the toilets. "Quit stalling, Riss. What do you mean about losing your scholarship?"

Her sigh was barely perceptible through the earbuds, but I knew that dramatic flair well. "I have an appointment I'm not going to make."

I loosened my grip on the mop. Dramatic, as usual. People didn't lose scholarships over a missed massage appointment. "So, call the client and reschedule like a responsible adult."

The gym's front door lock clicked and the door opened, allowing the bright morning light to stream in. One all-too-familiar, scuffed-up combat boot snuck in before the door could close again.

Frankie propped the door open with her hip and wiggled

her way through, carrying a stack of boxes. On top of the stack, two steaming styrofoam coffee cups perched precariously.

How she managed to not drop anything was a mystery.

Francine Delgado—Frankie to almost everyone but the cops—was my boss and the owner of this gym. It wasn't your typical gym, though, not the kind with those expensive machines and fancy yoga studios.

No, Subliminal was a boxing gym and home to a fight club for people like us—supernaturally Gifted.

It was also just plain home to Marissa and me.

The door swung shut behind Frankie, and the lock reengaged, dimming the gym again. Black paint covered all the windows and the front door for two primary purposes: keeping prying non-magical eyes from seeing what they shouldn't if the fae glamour disguising the building failed, and keeping the place from getting too hot during humid D.C. summers.

Keeping a place like this cool enough was expensive, no matter the time of year. We cut costs where we could, and thankfully, I was well-adjusted to the constant reek of body odor, among other nefarious scents.

"I can't just reschedule this appointment, Bree," Marissa said, so aghast you'd think I'd asked her to chop someone's head off. "They said this client is super important. A VIP."

"Coffee?" Frankie's voice was filled with gravel from years of smoking as she strode around the boxing ring toward me.

The ring took up a good chunk of the gym's center, while weight benches, weights, punching bags, climbing ropes, and other random equipment were scattered around any remaining open space in small clusters. At first glance, it probably looked like a mishmash of random placements, but our regulars preferred it that way.

As Frankie approached, the stack of boxes covered most of her face, but somehow, she hadn't dropped the coffee cups yet. I knew my boss was dexterous for her age, but this was impressive even for her.

Her combat boots left tracks through the wet cement floor, which was par for the course. These floors would be disgusting again in just a few hours.

When Frankie reached me, she paused to peek around the boxes. Her dark grey and white hair swept her chin in a frizzy mess of curls that she rarely tried to control, and today's jeans included so many rips and tears, I wasn't sure they could be called fashionable anymore.

"If they're so VIP, why can't you make it?" I pointed to my earbud after Frankie shot me a confused look. "Marissa."

"Is that Frankie?" My sister's voice suddenly perked up. "Tell her hi and thanks for the advice."

I eyed Frankie suspiciously. "Tell her yourself when you get here for your super important appointment. And what advice?"

Chuckling, the gym owner shook her head before disappearing into her office. After a decade of us living under her roof, she was well-accustomed to our sibling banter.

I dipped the mophead into the yellow bucket of brownish-white water. The bubbles were long gone. Almost time to get fresh water and soap. I'd mopped half the gym already, one of my many tasks to keep this place up and running and off the city inspector's list.

Bodily fluids left unattended were a bit of a no-no for businesses these days, Gifted or otherwise.

"Nothing you need to worry about," Marissa said. "Anyway, I *may* have miscalculated the time I'd need to get there."

"Wait, is it today?"

"Um, did I not mention that?"

As I lifted the dripping mop into the bucket's wringer, I paused, my skin prickling with goosebumps. You could get almost anywhere in DC within an hour. "Marissa, where are you?"

"There was a party last night at a private estate in Virginia. Oh, Bree, you should see this place," she said in a rush. "It's absolutely gorgeous and—"

"You better not be asking what I think you're asking."

"Bree, you have to," she pleaded.

Shaking my head, I pushed the wringer's lever, squeezing out the excess water from the mop head. "No, I'm not covering for you again. Call and reschedule."

"You don't understand." Her guilty conscience was audible through the phone. "I will definitely lose my scholarship."

"That's a harsh punishment for missing one client's massage." I slapped the mop back onto the cement floor and didn't even grimace when murky droplets hit my faded overalls —they'd seen worse.

The silence stretched until it clicked.

I groaned and leaned my forehead against the mop's handle. "Riss...how many jobs have you missed?"

"Um, I mean, who's even counting? It's a stupid rule anyway. I should be able to set my own hours, but the school constantly books these early ones without asking me."

Only my sister could make following the rules sound so offensive. "And what time is this appointment exactly?"

There was a slight pause before she said, "Just remember this could cost me everything, Ree. Danielle said she'd have no choice but to cancel my scholarship if it happened again."

My heart dropped into my stomach, and I closed my eyes.

She only called me Ree when she was desperate to get her way, and I was such a sucker about it because it was what our mother had called me.

Marissa had barely been old enough to remember her when she died, but I'd told my sister enough stories to fuel her imagination. Ree and Riss, her heart and soul.

Guilt gripped my insides and held on tight. I'd promised my mother that I would protect my little sister, and I would fulfill that promise no matter the cost. I owed her that much.

After all, it was my fault she'd died.

I clenched my teeth together. We couldn't pay for her massage therapy school without that scholarship. Money wasn't exactly easy to come by when you had to hide your Gifts.

"What time?" I asked, resigned.

"Ten."

I glanced at my watch. "Marissa! That is in 30 minutes!" Throwing my hands up, I nearly dropped the mop. I scrambled to catch the handle before it clattered to the floor. "I'm not even done mopping."

"I'll clean twice for you, I promise." Excitement filled her tone. She knew she'd won.

"Three times," I said sternly.

"That seems excessive."

"Three or no deal."

"How about two and a free massage?" A distinct whine tinted her tone. She hated cleaning more than I did.

I mean, who actually *liked* cleaning?

"My massages are always free. Three or I'm hanging up."

She sighed. "Fine."

"This is the last time. I mean it. I can't keep bailing you out."

Marissa's squeal of delight nearly burst my eardrums. "You really are the best big sister ever. I'll send you the address. Just pretend you're me, and it'll go great. Love you, bye!"

And there it was—the familiar cycle of bailing her out, followed by promises of repayment that rarely came to fruition.

Why did I let her do this to me? How did she always get away with this crap?

The answer was simple: I was such a pushover.

I tugged my phone out of my pocket and waited for the address. If I could have afforded a new one, I would've thrown the traitorous device against the wall and pretended like I never got her message. Since I couldn't afford it, I settled for glaring ferociously at the background picture of Marissa and me making silly faces at each other.

I wasn't mad, per se. This was far from the first time she'd behaved this way. Taking me for granted and whatnot.

No, not mad—I was disappointed.

Yeesh. Talk about becoming our father.

Swallowing hard against the sudden lump in my throat, I banished those thoughts back out to sea where they belonged. I'd chosen to leave and would bear the cost for the rest of my life. Anything to give Marissa a true chance at a free life, to choose whether she'd get married and to whom.

We would be stronger than the tide no matter where we lived.

My phone buzzed as her text came through with the client's address. I plugged it into the maps app and groaned. Great. It was down in the Wharf, and there was no way I'd make it on time unless I left two minutes ago.

Better late than never. I was sure I could fake some tears if it came down to it.

CHAPTER 2

Dominic

Dominic sat in an oversized brown leather chair facing his grandfather's desk and the wizened man behind it. Both men had assumed a demeanor of cold indifference, a look Dominic had perfected after years of getting beaten into submission until it was second nature.

By the man in front of him, no less.

Despite his grandfather's smaller frame, there was a reason Ichiro Sato was on top of the food chain, and it wasn't due to his age.

"Kill or be killed" was the Sato family motto, and his grandfather, uncles, aunts, cousins, and every other extended family member lived it to its fullest, including Dominic. Which meant he'd learned to take a beating early on if he wanted to survive long enough to take over the family business.

Ichiro's office sat on the top floor of one of the most expensive buildings in downtown Washington, D.C. As had become general practice over the years, the Sato family purchased the entire building to keep prying eyes—human or Gifted—out of their many businesses.

Antique furniture, rare artifacts, and mahogany book-shelves filled with first editions decorated the room, each item a symbol of power and wealth. Their morning shadows stretched across the polished wood floor.

And yet, Dominic found the luxurious room and its primary inhabitant suffocating.

As Ichiro listened to Aaron going over the latest inventory reports and expenses incurred, he steepled his fingers beneath his bare chin. The old man had started shaving his face as well as his head long before Dominic was born, and his pale skin gleamed beneath the office lights.

Aaron, the man speaking, was one of Dominic's closest friends and someone he could rely on no matter the situation. Since loyalty wasn't an easy commodity to come by in their world, once you found it, you never let go.

With bright blond hair and baby blue eyes, Aaron wasn't part of the Sato family by blood, but he'd crept his way into all their hearts years ago. It helped that Aaron was one of the best accountants money could buy, and the Sato family had obscene amounts of money to buy whatever they wished, people or otherwise.

Business was great, just not always legal by human or Gifted standards.

"What about the crates from South Africa?" Ichiro asked. "Any issues with customs?"

Aaron smirked, displaying the dimples that had women of all ages swooning anywhere he went. "Not a single issue. That new witch you brought in has become quite the valuable asset with slipping past borders."

Although his grandfather's face remained stoic and impassive, Dominic was well-versed in the man's micro-movements.

Approval glinted in the old man's dark brown eyes faster than one could blink.

"Your marketing efforts have been lacking, Dominic." Ichiro scrutinized the documents before him. "Or perhaps it's just your commitment to this family that's lacking."

Dominic's fists tightened, his dragon spirit stirring within him like a restless storm, and tension crackled in the air like electricity. Biting back a retort, he forced himself to maintain control. He knew better than to challenge Ichiro in front of Aaron.

That time would come.

He flashed a charming yet repentant smile that always worked in his favor. "I'll work on that, sir."

The room's suffocating atmosphere amplified with each passing second, highlighting Dominic's feeling of isolation within his own family. As one of the potential heirs to take over the empire, he had never fit the mold his grandfather had crafted for him, always struggling beneath the weight of the old man's impossible expectations.

Every day of his life, Dominic strove to prove he deserved to be there, needed to if he wanted to achieve his goal. Except a lingering sense of uncertainty had started to grow over the past year. Even now, as they discussed the intricacies of the family's businesses and clients he was expected to oversee directly one day, he questioned where his loyalties should lie.

For now, he would stick to the plan that had been years in the making. He would watch and wait.

Behind him, the door swung open and thundering footsteps barged in. Dominic didn't need to turn around to know it was Kenzo—only his youngest cousin stomped around like a gargoyle—but he did so anyway, swiftly coming to his feet in a feigned display of protection.

Aaron did the same, their two bodies effectively blocking the old man behind the desk from view. Failing to protect the empire's patriarch from an attack was a death sentence.

Not that the old man needed protection.

Kenzo sauntered into the room without so much as an apologetic smile for the intrusion. He opened his mouth to speak but stopped when he came face-to-face with Aaron and Dominic, and his eyes narrowed with suspicion. Like most of the Sato family, Kenzo had jet-black hair, dark brown eyes, and lighter, almost pale white skin.

Only Dominic had a deeper bronze hue to his skin due to his father's Brazilian ethnicity, and Dominic's was the only untraditional name. If he hadn't known better, he would have thought his parents had hated him.

He turned his head slightly to glance at his grandfather. An interruption without knocking as Kenzo had just done would come with a harsh punishment. Disrespect wasn't permitted in the Sato family.

Unless it was directed at Dominic, of course.

But as usual, once Ichiro realized it was Kenzo, his tensed shoulders relaxed. Behind his thin wire spectacles, crinkles formed as he smiled at one of his favorite grandsons.

"Apologies, *ojisan*," Kenzo said, though his sarcastic tone spoke otherwise. He strolled forward as if he owned the place, his oversized blue jumpsuit swishing with each step. "I didn't realize you had visitors."

Ah, yes, Dominic thought with annoyance as he took his seat again. *Visitors.*

Despite the differences in how he was treated compared to

his cousins and any other family members, Dominic still desired his grandfather's approval. It was ludicrous. He was much too independent and successful to care about an old man's feelings, especially this man's. The Sato family patriarch was the Devil incarnate.

And yet.

It didn't matter that Dominic bonded with one of the strongest, most powerful dragons their family had ever known. It didn't matter how much money and fame, or how much honor he brought to the Sato name.

He was a bastard.

That was all he'd ever be to this family, all thanks to his mother's decision to follow her heart rather than obey her father's command.

Dominic didn't fault his mother. He'd never known the woman. She'd died during childbirth, a sign everyone took to prove she'd made the wrong choice. Her reckless behavior brought shame to the family name, and she'd paid the price with her life.

So why was Dominic still paying for her sins?

Because Ichiro also blamed the poor, defenseless babe that came from her womb. The baby should have died, not grandfather's precious Fumiko, and Dominic was a constant reminder of his loss.

The old man had taken Dominic in after his father died, which was a small mercy on good days; a terrible mistake on the worst. Someday, he would give Ichiro exactly what he deserved.

Dominic took a deep breath and released it through his nose slowly, calming his racing pulse. He'd learned that trick to conquer fear and pain during his early years of fighting in the ring. Stirring up old memories wouldn't do anyone any good, least of all him.

"You know better than to come in without knocking," Ichiro chided Kenzo. "You're lucky you're a Sato."

Out of the corner of his eye, Dominic caught Aaron's eye roll. He knew as well as anyone what his grandfather meant. Dominic might have carried the Sato surname now after Ichiro legally changed it, but he had been born a Costa.

His grandfather had kept Dominic's first name as a constant reminder of his mother's betrayal.

Regardless, Dominic would have received twenty lashes for the same mistake his cousin just made. Even some of the other family members would have gotten a tongue-lashing.

But not Kenzo.

No, not the golden child that could do no wrong despite fucking up time and again.

Kenzo was flashy and arrogant, his flamboyant attire clashing with the room's austere ambiance. Dominic could never understand what his grandfather saw in Kenzo. To him, there was nothing but a distinct sense of undeserved superiority. Even his dragon was useless, barely able to keep his charge out of trouble.

Kenzo smiled smugly and ran the tip of his tongue across the gold grills covering his front teeth. "Lucky indeed."

"Well, why have you barged in like a barbarian?" Ichiro asked.

"Ben, that pawnshop owner over on Rhode Island Ave., is behind on his payment." Kenzo's dark brown eyes glinted with promised violence. "I want to pay him a visit before he can skip town."

Ichiro raised an eyebrow. "You're not a collector."

No, that delightful job was left to someone like Dominic.

"This guy owes me personally, too." Kenzo shrugged. "Two birds, one stone."

Ichiro considered him for a moment before giving a curt nod. "Very well then."

Kenzo's face lit up with cruel excitement as he bowed. "Thank you, *ojisan*."

At least the idiot had that much common sense.

As Kenzo turned to leave, Ichiro's voice cracked out like a whip. "Take Dominic with you."

Dominic's stomach curdled. He should have known better than to think he'd be off the hook.

His cousin's mouth dropped open. "But I—"

Ichiro's sharp gaze fixed on Kenzo and a red hue flashed behind his eyes. He rarely released his dragon these days, but he also had no need. Memories of the vicious beast kept most people in line. "You question my decision?"

Kenzo snapped his mouth shut and bowed his head, but anger radiated off him in near-tangible waves. "No, *ojisan*."

Ichiro nodded and shooed them away with a hand.

Knowing better than to argue, Dominic met Aaron's humorously pitied look. His friend knew he would be babysitting his cousin during the entire collection.

As he followed Kenzo from the room, his dragon spirit—known as Joubunaryūō, or Jou for short—writhed within, mirroring his tumultuous emotions. Wisps of power coalesced around him as barely visible tendrils of crimson light that echoed the flames of defiance burning inside.

There was only one way out of this family—death.

The only question was whose.

CHAPTER 3

Dominic

"I don't want to be here anymore than you do," Dominic ground out between his teeth, Jou churning within him like a hungry flame.

As if having to tag along on this collection wasn't bad enough, his cousin had complained about Dominic being there the entire twenty-minute drive through D.C. traffic, away from the city center. Droning the kid out was easy, but it didn't make the experience any less painful.

As they exited Kenzo's ostentatious sports car, his cousin blew out a breath. "Fine. Whatever. Just follow my lead and stay out of my way."

He didn't bother with a response. What Kenzo wanted didn't matter. This was a babysitting job, which meant his grandfather expected Dominic to step in if necessary. Correction—*when* necessary.

Taking in the rundown strip mall they'd parked in front of, he frowned. The location was not ideal. They were exposed, surrounded by the constant bustle of humanity. As long as

Kenzo kept his temper in check and this Ben character valued his life, they shouldn't draw too much attention to their visit.

But if there was one thing Dominic was certain of, it was that Kenzo would fuck this simple job up. The only unknown was how.

Kenzo led them to a dingy pawnshop, where the acrid stench of desperation and despair wafted from the building. A hodgepodge of trinkets, tarnished silverware, and dusty electronics sprawled across the window display. The window itself was covered with rusted bars and so much dust and cobwebs, most people would likely assume the place was closed, for the day or maybe forever.

They stepped inside, and a bell jingled above the door. A man with unkempt brown hair stood behind the counter, his gaze darting around the room. His faded shirt was wrinkled and hung loosely around his neck as if he'd grabbed it from the dirty laundry bin.

A nervous twitch plagued him, evident in the way his fingers tapped along the counter, drumming a subtle rhythm of restlessness. The counter was cluttered with crumpled papers and objects.

When the man's gaze landed on Kenzo, his eyes widened and his fingers ceased their endless tapping.

This must be the man of the hour.

Expecting the shopkeeper to bolt, Dominic locked the front door and switched off the open sign. Kenzo was by the man's side in the blink of an eye.

"I didn't want to have to come here, Bennie-boy." Kenzo stepped closer, boxing the man in behind the counter. "But I don't appreciate having my things stolen."

"Please," Ben begged, his Adam's apple bobbing with a gulp, "I didn't know."

Kenzo chuckled.

Dominic was sure his cousin meant the laugh to be a dark and deadly sound. But coming from him it sounded comical, like he was holding back a cough.

"I wish I believed that." Kenzo leaned his arm against the cluttered counter and nearly lost his balance when a pile of papers slipped beneath him. He righted himself and adjusted the gold chains around his neck. "Except everyone knows I own the pyrocrystal supply around here. No selling without my express permission, and you don't have my permission, do you?"

Dominic stilled, unease prickling along his scalp. If Ichiro had known this "personal collection" of Kenzo's was drug-related, he never would have let his favorite grandson tag along. Drug addicts were notoriously unstable, and addictions to pyro-crystals had devastating consequences for everyone around them.

The drug had only become accessible to non-dragons within the last few months, and no one seemed to know how or even why. Ichiro hadn't been overly concerned, so Dominic hadn't thought much more about it. He had other priorities that required his full attention.

But as the name implied, pyrocrystals were created with fire, a very specific type of fire.

A dragon's spirit-bonding ceremony was similar to a wolf shifter's, except wolves paired with their two-legged counter-parts just after a baby's birth. Doing so allowed the wolves a complete shift from one shape to the other at will. The shifters could also communicate with their wolves directly, and they had no need for tattoos.

Dragons were kept on a much tighter leash due to their more aggressive and violent tendencies. During a dragon's ceremony, a dragon paired with its chosen shifter via tattoo, which tethered the spirit's will to its host's. Subduing the ferocious beasts in this way meant communication was limited to emotions rather than direct communication like the wolves.

The magic involved in a fire dragon's pairing generated the pyrocrystals as a sort of residue, granting the new charge enhanced abilities when ingested. They were highly protected within the fire dragon community—until recently.

The sickly sweet scent of Ben's desperation grew. "Please, Kenzo, I swear I'll pay you back. Just give me a little more time. I'm working on a deal that—"

Dominic stepped forward, ethereal wisps of power coiling around his body like deadly serpents ready to strike. His voice was low and sharp as his dragon spirit awakened within him. "Enough. We came for the Sato money, plain and simple. Finish the job, Kenzo, or I will."

Despite his words, he couldn't deny the savage joy that rose with the thought of unleashing his power. He clenched his jaw, struggling to restrain the beast inside, and waited. The choice, as always, was up to the debtor.

Pay up, or face the consequences.

A mix of shame and defiance crossed Kenzo's expression. He had to have known he crossed a line by not revealing the truth to Ichiro, but the kid couldn't help himself.

"Look, I don't want any trouble." Ben swallowed hard and shoved his hands in his pockets. "I'll get you the money as soon as I can, I promise."

"Kenzo, get down!" Dominic barked out just as the man withdrew his hand and gulped the red crystal down.

Amazingly, his cousin listened. Most likely because the selfish brat valued his life more than his pride, or perhaps because he was too stunned to argue.

The shopkeeper's pupils dilated, and his eyes glowed like embers in a dying fire. A swirling vortex of unfathomable energy grew in each of his palms.

The crack of snapping wood echoed through the store as nearby objects burst into flames under the searing heat of the magical blaze. A massive fireball erupted from the shopkeeper's raised hands, illuminating everything in its path with an infernal light.

Dominic's lips curled into a predatory smile as he absorbed the fireball's impact, his dragon-hardened skin shielding him from harm. His back burned like the flames of Hell as Jou's essence emerged from his tattoo, a phantom specter enveloping his body in a fiery, otherworldly aura. Power surged through his veins and crackled under his skin in a web of crimson light.

With a thunderous roar, Dominic unleashed a counter-attack, and his dragon lunged forward.

Ben attempted to evade, but his movements were that of an amateur, feeble and inadequate. The dragon's claws sliced through the man's pitiful defenses, leaving deep, crimson gashes across his chest.

A cry of anguish tore from his lips as he staggered backward, his eyes wide with terror. He was finding out the hard way that pyrocrystals were no match for a real dragon.

With his dragon poised for another strike, Dominic closed the distance between them, a primal hunger fueling his steps.

His fangs elongated with malicious intent, ready to deliver the final, devastating blow.

"Please, no more." Ben's voice shook with desperation, and his flames fizzled into smoke.

The scent of fear permeated the air, mingling with the pungent fumes of urine.

Dominic paused, momentarily captivated by the terror that radiated from his prey. His instincts warred with a shred of lingering compassion, but his dragon's dominance prevailed. He thirsted for blood.

Surging forward, he pinned Ben against the wall by his throat. His lips pulled back from his fangs as he eyed the man's pulsing veins. "You shouldn't borrow money you have no intention of repaying. Be grateful we're not taking more."

A wretched cry escaped Ben's mouth before he fainted.

Dominic dropped the broken man and loomed over him, his chest heaving as he wrestled control back from the dragon. The intoxicating scent of blood lingered in the air and rendered the task near impossible.

Dismissing the man on the floor with a final flick of its tail, Jou swirled back around Dominic and reabsorbed into his tattoo.

Kenzo smirked, apparently satisfied with the outcome, but his eyes narrowed at Dominic as if to say he could have handled the situation himself. Except his reckless behavior had potentially put them all in danger, jeopardizing their business and their lives.

As they left the pawnshop and walked toward the car, a storm brewed beneath Dominic's composed exterior. Was using Joubunaryūō's powers the best way to handle that situation?

The fear in the debtor's eyes haunted him, reminding him

of the consequences that came with wielding such a lethal weapon, and the life he couldn't escape. The familiar weight of guilt settled in his chest.

No matter how much he struggled internally against his family's corrupt ways, in the end, he always found himself dragged back into their darkness. A darkness he craved as much as he loathed.

Was securing his place within the Sato family truly worth sacrificing his integrity?

How long could he walk this razor's edge before it slashed him to pieces?

CHAPTER 4

Bree

After plopping the mop back into the yellow bucket, I wheeled the ancient contraption over to the wall and stuck my head in Frankie's office. Although, it was more of an oversized closet than an office. There was enough room for a desk, a small fridge, and not much else.

"Hey Frankie, I have to bail Rissa out again. She promised three cleanings to make up for it. Don't let me forget to cash in, okay?"

My boss chuckled and glanced at me over her bright pink reading glasses. She was like the fifty-something-year-old woman who refused to get bifocals even though she desperately needed them. Except she was fae so she would never need them. "Not that you'll need the reminder, but sure thing, kid. Oh, and next time? Try sayin' no."

Frankie knew as well as I did how hard it was to say no to my little sister. It was a magic Marissa held over everyone she met and had absolutely nothing to do with being a siren.

I nodded and rushed toward the basement door, marked by

a bright red "Do Not Enter" sign. Since I was in a hurry, I shoved the door open and jumped over the handrail rather than take the five steps leading down to the basement floor.

The layout was more of a split-level than basement, but the whole building sat on the side of a hill, which meant most of the lower level was underground. Our space was nothing fancy —a far cry from the luxurious life we used to know.

Two cots, mine covered with books and Marissa's littered with clothes, were pushed against opposite walls. Two plastic bins sat beside each cot, acting as both dressers and nightstands and overflowing with our meager belongings.

A curtain provided a false sense of privacy for our bathroom, which contained little more than a shower, pedestal sink, and a toilet that clogged constantly. We could always use the locker room upstairs, but sometimes a girl needed a toilet to call her own.

The walk-up back door provided us with an escape route if needed, like those times when I didn't want to stop and chat with gym members on my way to the grocery store. Although it mostly served as Marissa's way of sneaking in and out after hours.

No windows, frequent leaks, and banging pipes made the open room Rissa and I called home feel like a basement—or even a dungeon. But we didn't complain. Not outside this room, anyway. Ten years ago, after finding me about to steal fish from a human vendor, Frankie offered us a place to live without hesitation.

Growing up in an underwater palace and society without having to worry about money hadn't given us the education needed to survive on land, especially since our father despised humankind. But I was a quick learner—unless it came to electronics—and determined to stay, so I'd accepted Frankie's offered hospitality.

Plus, we had nowhere else to go.

Frankie lived above the gym in a one-bedroom apartment that cost just shy of an arm and a leg each month. It provided us with a communal kitchen whenever a microwave wouldn't do. Her place was too small to sleep three people comfortably long-term and stank of decades worth of cigarette smoke.

The basement was the next best option, and over the years, we'd made it our own. Multicolored string lights gave the space a cozy feel, and various pictures and framed motivational quotes covered the walls.

I rummaged through the plastic bin that acted as my sister's dresser and pulled out one of her clean massage school uniforms. Since I had no time for a shower, I whipped on some deodorant, changed, and gathered up her equipment—a fold-up massage table and a bag full of things like towels, candles, and oils.

With everything in hand, I glanced forlornly at the book waiting on my pillow. The cover had fallen off before I'd gotten my hands on it at the used bookstore, and the pages were yellowing and dog-eared from previous owners.

Despite the book's ragged appearance, the author had crafted an amazing story I struggled to put down each night. I was so close to finding out whether the thief and agent defied the odds and fell in love by the end, but that answer would have to wait until later.

Oh, who was I kidding? It was a romance, of course they'd get together.

But the tension was to die for.

Snapping myself out of the wistful daydream, I rushed toward the basement's back door. Movement in my periphery stopped me short, and I grimaced. I couldn't believe I'd almost forgotten to tell Finley where I was headed.

At the surface of a fish tank—one of the few material items I ever spent money on—an axolotl bobbed his head up and down. Finley was a *luminara axolotl*, a rare species of salamander with magical abilities, and this particular little fellow had followed Marissa and me from home despite my command to stay.

I thanked Tethys every day he had disobeyed.

Opalescent scales that shimmered like moonlit pearls covered the creature's slender form, casting an ethereal glow in the aquarium waters. His iridescent skin transitioned seamlessly through a myriad of colors, from lustrous blues and purples to delicate shades of silver and gold, as if reflecting the enchantments of the mystical realm his species came from.

Intricate patterns decorated his body, dancing and shifting with every movement. They were ancient arcane symbols that wove tales of forgotten secrets and wisdom of ages past. On either side of his head, fringed, pearlescent pink gills fluttered like gossamer ribbons and highlighted his pale blue eyes.

He was the most adorable thing to ever exist on this planet, I was sure of it.

"Sorry, Finley." I stroked his slick skin with a fingertip. "I have to leave you behind today, but I'll be back soon."

The axolotl tilted his head, fluttering his gills with apparent disappointment. He let out a soft, melodic sound that conveyed his longing to join me.

"I know, buddy," I said with a sympathetic smile. "But this is an appointment I can't miss and you can't come to. It's important for Marissa. I'll make it up to you, I promise."

Finley blinked his large, round eyes and gave a small nod, understanding my words. He dove into the water and seaweed and playfully wiggled his tail, trying to lighten the mood.

"Behave while I'm gone, okay?" Smiling at his antics, I gave him a little wave. "No causing chaos or messing with Frankie's things. We don't want to piss her off do we?"

The axolotl gazed up at me with an adorably innocent expression, as if to assure me that he would be on his best behavior. I longed for the days when we could communicate telepathically underwater, but I knew he would stay put. As long as I promised to always come back.

"I'll bring you a treat when I get home. Maybe some of those delectable water bugs you love so much."

With that, I high-tailed it out the back door. The massage table was portable, but it was also much larger than a purse and unwieldy, not to mention heavy. I winced as the table bounced off the door frame with a bang and hoped I hadn't done any damage to it.

The door, that is, because I'd have to pay to fix it and funds were limited enough as it was. Marissa could deal with any fallout from any damaged equipment. It was her fault I was involved in this mess.

As I took the steps up to street level two at a time, I glanced at my watch. Twenty-four minutes to go. I could make it in twenty minutes easy without all this extra baggage weighing me down.

Downtown D.C. during springtime was a busy place. Add

in the hulking massage table thrown over my shoulder and I was a walking wrecking ball. The damn thing thumped against my back and legs the whole way, sure to give me more than a few bruises.

Thanks a lot, Riss.

Most people scurried out of my way as soon as they saw me coming. Those who didn't move yelled at me after I knocked into them. I ignored them like any other respectable D.C. citizen would do. These were the hazards of living in a city.

When I was forced to stop at a busy red light, a prickling sensation crawled across the back of my neck. It had become more common in recent days, making me feel like I was being watched.

I mean, lots of people were around who might be looking my way, but this was a more direct feeling. Almost sinister.

I glanced over my shoulder, but, just like all the other times, no one out of the ordinary stood out. You would think that the longer we were away from home, the less I would worry about our father finding us, dragging us back, and selling us off like prized cattle.

Unfortunately, my nerves had only gotten worse over the past ten years. Our luck had to be running out by now.

As soon as the light turned green, I hustled across the street and followed my phone's map directions to the building in question. I squinted up at the sign. This was one of the nicest condo buildings in the city. Maybe *the* nicest for all I knew. I wasn't rich anymore and never on land, so clamshells if I knew.

I yanked open the glass door and nearly ran into a nicely dressed couple about to exit. They stepped back as I struggled through the door. Except sudden resistance wrenched me back and threatened to dislodge my shoulder—the table had gotten stuck in the frame.

Muttering a few colorful obscenities I'd learned over the years at the gym, I turned the massage table so it could fit through the door. The couple exchanged a knowing, condescending look before exiting.

No, no, please don't worry about me, I thought with an eye roll. *I wouldn't want you to break a nail or something by helping the help.*

I ran up to the check-in counter completely out of breath.

A white-haired woman with leathery, tanned skin stared down her nose at me and raised an equally white eyebrow. "May I help you?"

"Br—Marissa Johnson... Here...for appointment... Number 2015. Nine o'clock," I said in gulping puffs.

Of course, Johnson was just a fake last name we'd chosen years ago. Our kind didn't need more than one name but paperwork on land demanded it.

Her shrewd gaze flicked to the computer screen and then back to me. "You're ten minutes late."

You know what? I changed my mind. Punching babies was for the weak. I wanted to brawl with a shark or a dragon, something that could fight back.

I pointed to the three elevators. "So, should I just go up then?"

The receptionist held up a bony finger and pressed a button on the computer. After a moment, she said, "Ms. Johnson is here for an appointment."

No one else was around, so I assumed—and hoped—she had on earbuds I couldn't see.

"Yes, sir." She pursed her lips, then typed something into

the computer. One of the elevator doors dinged and opened. "He's waiting for you."

As much as I tried to understand human world technology, I just couldn't wrap my brain around it all. How did a little machine make an elevator work like magic? Their wires didn't even connect anywhere.

By the time I clambered into the lift, I was a sweaty, swampy mess. The shiny steel walls reflected my face as well as a mirror, and I muttered at my flushed skin and the dark red frizz refusing to obey the hair spray around my hairline.

It was early spring, which meant snow was still possible despite the increasing warmth. Yet here I was, drenched in sweat, heading to one of Marissa's VIP clients.

Fabulous.

The receptionist's voice called out as the elevator door started to close, "I wouldn't recommend being late again. He doesn't appreciate having to wait."

Rolling my eyes for the second time in less than five minutes, which might have been a new record for me, I glanced at the rows of buttons. No one appreciated waiting, myself included. I realized I didn't know where I was headed. "What floor?"

The button for the penthouse was already lit.

As the door slid shut and the elevator whirred with movement, I let out a small groan. Of course the super-important client would own the penthouse. How silly of me not to realize that sooner.

I wiped my clammy palms against my pants. This was such a bad idea. I wasn't a masseuse, not even a real student. The little that I knew came from getting massages from Marissa and covering for her a handful of times.

I didn't even know who this client was, but they were sure to know I was a phony.

Maybe I could pretend to trip and twist my ankle or something...

The elevator dinged, interrupting my thoughts, and the doors slid open again. My eyebrows shot toward my hairline.

Holy coconuts, Catwoman.

CHAPTER 5
Bree

I stepped off the elevator and straight into a world of filthy-rich opulence. The moment I crossed the threshold, the sheer grandeur of the condo overwhelmed my senses.

Glossy white tile stretched out before me, the floor's polished surface reflecting the glow of recessed lighting above. The walls, painted in a sophisticated and understated shade of grey, exuded an air of refinement and elegance. Both the floors and walls served as a subtle backdrop, allowing the true stars of the space to shine.

And what stars they were.

Floor-to-ceiling windows covered the far side of the living room, commanding attention with their expansive presence. They framed a breathtaking view of the Potomac River, which had been transformed into a river of liquid gold by the mid-morning sun. The glimmering ripples danced and sparkled, casting a spell of enchantment upon the entire living space.

No one greeted me, so I clunked my way over and stood gaping at the beautiful scene below. The sight was nothing short of mesmerizing, as if the river itself had been carefully sculpted to enhance the condo's already lavish atmosphere.

As I stood there, captivated, a mix of awe and envy swirled within me. This was a place where dreams came to life, where the boundaries of possibility dissolved in the face of grandeur.

This client's life was a stark contrast to the humble space I called home, a visual, *visceral* reminder of the chasm that existed between the world of haves and have-nots. Taking a deep breath, I reminded myself why I was there.

I'd left a life of luxury behind, and now I had a job to do.

"Ms. Johnson?" a man's gruff voice asked, startling me so much I nearly fell over.

My plan for tripping and twisting my ankle might work out after all. The table banged against my hip, and I grimaced.

This was off to a fan-flipping-tastic start.

Tall and commanding, the man had a physique that hinted at hours spent honing his body to peak condition. His jawline was strong with a hint of dark stubble that added ruggedness to his otherwise refined appearance, and black hair framed his handsome face.

The man's dark-eyed gaze appraised me as if I were a potential threat. I couldn't tell what he thought of me, but I needed to pass the test.

I swiped strands of hair that had escaped my rushed ponytail out of my face and tried to smile. "Yep, that's me. Marissa Johnson, at your service, sir."

He frowned as if finding my answer odd.

I mean, my answer *was* odd. Who repeated their name like that?

This girl.

"You're late," he said.

Stating the obvious was turning into a real trend today. "Yes, well, I'm here now."

"Follow me."

Unfortunately, the man made no move to assist me with my things before turning around and walking away. Rich and polite didn't always go hand in hand. I lugged the giant table down a hallway and into an oversized bedroom.

The room was simply furnished considering the rest of the digs, but ultra-modern. A shiny black comforter covered a king-sized bed, hugged on either side by matching nightstands, and a mirror hung over a long dresser. No knick-knacks decorated any of the surfaces, and, other than the mirror, the walls were bare.

Like the living room, spotless floor-to-ceiling windows took up one entire wall and opened onto a large terrace. It was breathtaking.

What a lucky rich guy.

I wasn't bitter. I'd been born a princess after all, but I'd be lying if I said I didn't miss some of the luxuries.

"Set up there." The man gestured to a place close to the windows. "Mr. Sato will be here in a moment."

"Oh, I thought you were—" I turned to face him only to find myself talking to an empty room, "—the client."

Not that I was naïve enough to think he'd truly left me on my own. I was sure there were hidden cameras all over this place. The owner probably had nightly visitors sign waivers before getting down and dirty between the sheets.

Sighing, I set down my bag of supplies and got to work on the table. As I set up, I found myself glancing out the window every few seconds. The river water was rougher than usual today thanks to last night's rain, and I longed to feel its power rushing beneath my fingertips.

By the time ocean water flowed through the Chesapeake Bay and into the river, only a hint of salt remained. But that mere hint was like ecstasy to a fish out of water like me. Fresh water showers and our talismans were just enough to keep my sister and me from losing our minds from thirst.

I gripped the amulet dangling from my neck. The gem's weight against my chest was a constant reminder of the life I'd given up, a world to which I could never return. Not if I wanted to live free and make my own choices. And definitely not if I wanted that same life for Marissa.

When the table was set up, I spread two thin white sheets over top. Why these massage places always used white was beyond my understanding.

Sure it might've looked nice and clean, adding to the calm ambiance and all, but oil stains were hard to get out. The sun was a far better way to bleach stains than any detergent, but laying out sheets to catch some rays required more space than we had.

A bird flew by outside, catching my attention. As it dove toward the lapping waves, my gaze drifted to the water once again. I leaned forward, pressing my hands into the massage table to see better.

"You never get used to it."

I yelped and whirled to face the man who'd spoken. And then my mouth remained hanging open because this man was drop-dead gorgeous. If I thought the first guy was attractive, he was a lit match compared to this inferno of hotness. As in the most good-looking man I'd ever seen in my entire life.

He had to be a few inches over six feet tall and had a body any Subliminal fighter would kill for, or kill to touch. Sculpted yet lean muscles flexed beneath his bare chest as he adjusted his stance.

Naturally tanned skin—a color that would never grace my own sunburn-loving paleness—covered every inch of his exposed body. Which was quite a lot considering he only wore a pair of loose black sweatpants that hung low on his hips. His muscles were chiseled to perfection, each line of his toned, flat stomach and arms visible as if he'd been carved from stone by a master sculptor.

His stomach led to a deliciously indented V slipping below the top of his pants. My gaze must have lingered there a bit too long because he cleared his throat.

I forced my attention up to his face and could do nothing but stare. Black hair kept short on the sides but longer on top swept back from his forehead in a tousled yet fashionable look. I assumed it was fashionable since I didn't keep up with that sort of thing.

His eyes were absolutely mesmerizing. Irises the color of dark whiskey gazed back with an intensity that sent warmth pooling straight to my core.

He tucked his hands casually into his sweatpants' pockets and looked toward the water.

Wow. I'd never been stunned speechless by a guy before, but I guess there was a first time for everything.

And I completely forgot what he'd said. "Uh...what?"

Tides, Bree, pay attention. You've seen good-looking guys before.

He glanced down at me and drew his eyebrows together. His gaze roved over my face and body, all of which warmed. "The view."

Oh, right.

I nodded. "I'm sure It's one of a kind."

"You're late."

Yes, and currents are strong. Just in case I didn't know that tidbit as an adult able to read a clock, not one but two people in this building had already notified me of my lateness.

Be nice, Bree, I chided myself. Marissa might not get kicked out for missing an appointment any more, but offending a client could come with the same consequence.

"Please accept my apologies, Mr. Sato," I said demurely, dropping my gaze.

"Only if you call me Dominic."

Dominic.

The name struck a chord within me as though familiar somehow. I was pretty sure I'd never met anyone named Dominic, but maybe I'd seen his name somewhere. The luxurious digs hinted at the possibility of being someone important enough to be newsworthy.

"You can lie there on your stomach." I pointed to the massage table and crouched to get the supplies from my sister's bag. When I had everything in hand, I stood, turned around, and froze.

The handsome client had his naked back to me, about to climb onto the table. While his rounded butt was absolute perfection and worthy of a moment's appreciation, it was the massive tattoo of a red dragon sprawled across his entire back that stopped me in my tracks.

My heartbeat thumped wildly. I knew that tattoo almost as well as my own face. This wasn't just some random VIP.

This was the Red Dragon.

Mother of pearl...

Marissa's client was the Red Dragon? *The* Red Dragon?

Something clattered to the floor, and Dominic glanced over his shoulder. His gaze took in the dropped bottle at my feet before flicking up to meet my wide-eyed stare.

I recognized those eyes now, though I'd only ever seen them through a mask before today. During the illegal matches, Subliminal fighters wore magical masks to conceal their faces and identities, but many had other noticeable attributes like tattoos that they kept hidden when not in the ring.

But unlike all the other fighters, the Red Dragon never trained at Subliminal between fights. None of the dragons did; their beasts were too recognizable.

Dominic smirked, and I dropped my gaze to the floor, my cheeks growing hot.

Clearly, he had no concerns with me knowing his identity because this client, as in the man standing in front of me, was the most notorious, most lethal fighter ever to grace Subliminal's ring. He was a man I'd only gotten to watch fight from the shadows years ago, but I'd longed to be a part of that world ever since.

And now, I was about to touch him.

"Er, sorry," I mumbled and snatched up the dropped bottle.

Thank the tides it was plastic and not glass.

Ugh, when had I become so human?

The bed creaked and the sheets rustled as he got settled, sounds I should have noticed were absent before turning around the first time. Then again, I wasn't the one studying to become an actual masseuse.

"I'm sure you've seen plenty of naked men before in your line of work, no?"

My cheeks grew even hotter, sure to be flaming red by now. While it was most likely true Marissa had seen plenty of naked men doing this job—a thought I didn't want to pursue further —I didn't like the unintentional sexual innuendo.

Or maybe it was intended. The Red Dragon was well known for his conquests inside the ring *and* out, scenarios I'd often dreamed of being included in once upon a time. Until I'd realized he was nothing more than an egotistical, fin-licking barnacle who wouldn't give an adoring fan the time of day.

Whatever his intention, I chose to consider the question rhetorical. After taking a deep breath, I felt brave enough to lift my gaze again. He was on the bed face down, the top sheet draped over his bottom half.

I rolled my shoulders back, determined to get this over with and back to my real job. Unlike the sixteen-year-old version of myself who'd first laid eyes on Dominic Sato, I knew better than to ogle after playboys like him.

Besides, those toilets wouldn't clean themselves.

CHAPTER 6
Dominic

There was no denying the woman was beautiful. Almost otherworldly so. Her deep bluish-green eyes spoke of depths to rival the ocean's, and streaks of red and gold flashed in her dark brown hair as the morning sun caressed each strand.

But it wasn't the masseuse's beauty that had captured Dominic's interest when he saw her staring out the window. That wasn't the only thing, at any rate.

No, the calming sensation that washed over him the moment he entered the room was like nothing he'd experienced before. The feeling piqued his interest, enticing him to explore that sensation more.

The pink flush that swept over her face after seeing his naked body branded itself behind his closed eyelids, and he grinned against the massage table's face cushion. His amusement of her innocent reactions stirred the dragon within him awake, and his interest in her doubled as Jou's curiosity mixed with his.

The distinct sound of slick oil rubbing between hands

drifted closer as Marissa moved to stand at the head of the table. Her once white sneakers were covered in a layer of filth and—

Fuck me.

Dominic sucked in a breath as her palms touched his shoulders, and a surge of cool energy caressed his skin. Since their kind ran hot, his dragon rumbled his appreciation.

Her hands stilled. "Is everything okay?"

Fearing she'd remove her hands, he nodded and cleared his throat. "Just cooler than I expected."

That was such an understatement.

"Sorry," she said quietly. "It'll warm up as I go."

As she resumed the massage and pressed the heel of her palms into his muscles, her touch sent wave after wave of ocean breezes and deep waters over his skin. The more she touched him, the more he drowned in the sensations, and his eyelids fluttered shut.

Dominic had loved the ocean as a child and begged his father to take him to the Delaware beaches every summer. The waves there were as familiar to him as the man's face—one he made sure to never forget—and this woman's touch brought those memories rushing toward the surface with sparkling clarity.

"If you don't mind me asking," Marissa's soft voice slipped between the cracks of his consciousness, "why choose someone from a massage school? Considering your obvious success in life, I mean. You can afford the best."

With great difficulty, he pried his eyes open and focused on the lines of the floor. "That's quite the assumption."

Her hands paused on his arm. "Okay, but it's an accurate assumption."

He chuckled. Sassy, and he liked it. "Despite what you see, I know what it's like to start at the bottom. Someone helped me, and now I like to pay the favor forward."

While it was true that Ichiro Sato had taken Dominic in after his father's death, that didn't mean his grandfather had made it easy for him. Even though the old man owned most of the city's underground dealings, Dominic had to work for what he had just like anyone else.

Well, maybe not just like anyone else. Most people didn't have to break bones and spill blood to succeed in life. Not literally, anyway.

Satisfied with his answer, the pressure of her touch resumed. "Huh."

That certainly wasn't what he'd expected a woman in her shoes to say. Generous, maybe. Altruistic. Even chivalrous. "Huh?"

"It's just interesting."

That was more like it. "How's that?"

"Not many in your position would do the same."

"I presume most in my current position are too relaxed to think clearly," he said with a teasing note in his words. "Your touch is remarkable."

Once again, her hands stilled, the pressure lightening. "You know what I mean."

Not even a bashful thanks for the compliment? He must have been losing his touch. "Many wealthy people in this city didn't start at the bottom like you and me. It's hard to appreciate the climb if you've never had to make it."

She didn't respond, but thankfully, she didn't remove her hands either. Her cool touch continued to ease the tenseness in his muscles and mind, and Jou soon drifted back to sleep, rumbling softly.

Once again, Dominic floated in and out of his memories, contentment seeping into every pore as he lost himself in her touch. The sensations pulsed through him like gentle waves, continuing between his legs, where he felt himself stiffening.

This wasn't the only time he'd grown hard during a massage, but it took him a few moments of focus to realize she wasn't doing a very good job at the massage part. Not even for a student.

"How long have you been training to become a masseuse?" he asked as she moved down his arm.

"A few months."

So, either she was a terrible student or lying about how long she'd been training. Not that it mattered to him at this point.

She reached his hands, and an electric shock ran up to his shoulder. It wasn't painful, at least not in his arm. But his cock stiffened to painful proportions.

What in the hell was she doing to him?

Warm air kissed his skin as she pulled her hands away, and he wondered if she could tell he was so aroused. The sound of slick oil between her hands came again. The image of her naked and rubbing oil over his body before he made her come in a very different way flashed through his mind.

Dominic didn't usually have this kind of reaction toward women, not since he was a teenager unable to control himself. Beautiful women came and went from his life like fashionable clothes. Sometimes they suited him nicely for a while before their vibrancy faded or fell out of style.

Keeping them at arm's length was the easiest way to maintain his façade as a womanizer. If he ever hoped to convince Ichiro he was the right man to take over the Sato empire, he needed to keep his true intentions hidden. He couldn't let emotions interfere with his plans.

And that meant living a lie for the better part of a decade.

Coolness returned to his skin as Marissa's thumbs rubbed down his leg. A sharp pain shot through his calf, and sparks raced up his leg. He grunted as his muscles seized.

An emptiness filled his entire being as she snatched her hands away. "Oh! I'm so sorry."

Laughing, he flexed his foot to release the cramp. "Not your fault. I forgot to warn you it tends to do that."

"Your leg randomly goes hard as a rock?" she asked as she gently rubbed his calf.

It wasn't the only thing hard as a rock right now.

"It's from an old injury."

"From Subliminal?"

Dominic's body stilled as a primal instinct took over, preparing to fight. How did this woman know about Subliminal? The gym was strictly for the Gifted.

Was this massage a setup?

Was Ichiro finally putting the Sato bastard down?

"Subliminal?" he asked.

The masseuse's hands paused. "Er, sorry. Was I not supposed to know that? I just—it's just that I recognized your tattoo from when you used to fight."

While Dominic remained on edge, some of the tension eased from his body. Enough to encourage her to continue the massage. "You're a member?"

"Uh, yup."

Of all the things he expected from this curious creature, it wasn't an interest in boxing. "Small world."

Her laugh caught him off guard, cooling his body from the

inside out in a tantalizing way. "That's for sure. I won't say anything, if that's what you're worried about."

"It's not. The NDA you signed covers that."

"Oh, right. Duh." She slid her hands up to the top of the sheet and held it ever so slightly away from his body. "You can flip over now."

He turned over, grateful for the chance to study the exquisite details of her face.

She lowered the sheet and tucked it in around his body. As she did, the sheet tented above his erection. Her gaze flicked to it and a red flush overtook her cheeks and neck before she looked away again.

Dominic couldn't gauge whether her reaction was due to inexperience or innocence. "Lying here naked makes one rather vulnerable, doesn't it?"

She cleared her throat and pumped more oil into her palms. "Like you said, nothing I haven't seen before. No need to be embarrassed."

Amusement curled his lips into a smirk. "Do I look embarrassed to you?"

Her seafoam gaze met his, and he nearly drowned in those depths. She studied him for a heartbeat before saying, "No."

The remainder of the massage passed in comfortable silence, punctuated only by the occasional awkward fumble as her inexperienced hands worked over his muscles. Despite those moments, his body slowly melted into the table beneath him.

It was the best and worst massage he'd ever had, and it was over much too soon.

"Time's up," her melodic voice roused Dominic from his rest.

As Marissa moved away, wiping any remaining oil from her

hands on a clean cloth, he sat up and watched her work. There was something magical about the way she moved. Considering she knew who he was and was a Subliminal member, that meant she was Gifted as well.

He just couldn't tell what she was.

"That was incredible," he said genuinely. "Do you use your Gifts?"

She continued to pack up her things with her back facing him, but her shoulders tensed. "No. That was just a regular, plain old massage."

"Could have fooled me." Dominic slid off the massage table, dropping the sheet and pulling on his sweats. He knew she would be more prepared this time, but he'd half-hoped she would catch him naked again, only from the front. See what her touch did to him.

"Be sure to let the school know you were satisfied when you get the feedback form," Marissa said over her shoulder.

Far from satisfied, he was just tying the string of his pants when she turned to face him. Her gaze slid down the front of his body and snagged on the hard length straining against the fabric. Her throat bobbed as she gulped.

"I need...uh, to get the table," she stammered, her gaze flicking behind him.

He didn't move. "Sure thing."

She hesitated another moment before stepping around him, angling her body in a way that made it clear she didn't want to touch him. The only question was whether she was afraid of offending him or that she'd enjoy it. Likely the latter.

Turning to watch her pack up the table, he enjoyed the way the muscles along her toned arms and legs flexed and moved. Her boxing hobby was more obvious now.

She slung the table's bag over her shoulder, then reached for her supplies. "Did you know there was a Gifted masseuse at the school?"

"No, that was purely coincidental." But now that Dominic met her, he'd request her services every time. Just not because of her Gifted nature.

She glanced at the bedroom door. "Okay, well, um, bye."

Usually, he would head straight for the shower after a massage. But as Marissa left the room, he found himself following her. The words were out of his mouth before he'd even processed the thought. "How about a date?"

The question must have surprised them both. Her body tensed slightly but she didn't answer him until she reached the elevator and pushed the button. "That would be a hard nope."

"Why?"

She shrugged and then had to catch the strap before the giant bag fell off her shoulder. "I don't date clients."

The elevator door slid open and she stepped inside.

"Don't consider me a client then."

She pushed the lobby button. "No can do, I'm afraid. School rules, you know?"

The dragon inside him rolled over lazily and chuckled. They both knew there was no such rule, which meant...

Was she saying no to a date with Dominic Sato?

As the doors started to close, her lips curled up into a smile that set his pulse racing. She fluttered her fingers in a wave. "Toodles."

She disappeared as the doors slid shut.

Dominic stared at the elevator, stunned. This masseuse was very different from any others he'd flirted with in the past. It was as if she had woven some kind of spell around him, making him question everything he thought he knew about himself.

And then she'd turned him down.

Shaking his head, he forced himself to move away from the elevator and concentrate on the matters at hand. Getting side-tracked by a pretty face would only jeopardize his chances of gaining Ichiro's approval, if such a thing was possible in the first place.

And yet as he walked back toward his bedroom, the lingering scent of jasmine and salt-filled breezes followed him, teasing his senses and kindling the curiosity within him. He'd always been confident with women, but something about this one made him feel uncertain, vulnerable even.

No, with so much at stake, he couldn't allow distractions. He ran a hand through his hair, pushing thoughts of Marissa to the back of his mind and vowing to focus on what truly mattered—

Securing his future role as head of the Sato empire.

CHAPTER 7

Bree

I was always most at peace in the ocean. The waves enveloped me in a way only a lover could. Within those dark depths, I was weightless, breathless, yet full of life. The currents tugging me closer, willing me to let go. To abandon my control.

I longed to listen to the ocean's song, longed to add my voice to its choir again.

The call of the sea was almost too much to bear some days. And as the years dragged on, I wondered how much of it I had imagined. The ocean didn't really sing...

...did it?

A loud bang startled me from my reverie.

I blinked, and the bathroom stall swam back into focus. Handwritten notes and phone numbers marked the metal dividers separating the two stalls, and the once white tile floor had long since turned a gross shade of tan and dark brown. The grout needed a scrub—

Wait, no. Scratch that.

The entire bathroom needed demolition.

From my vantage point kneeling in front of the toilet,

holding a tattered sponge in one gloved hand and a label-less cleaning spray in the other, I had an up-close and personal view of the porcelain throne. Thankfully, the copious amount of bleach kept the worst smells from knocking me flat on my back.

None of the toilets in here had been replaced since at least the '80s. Maybe longer. Much like a tree stump, I imagined the rings in the bowls revealed the porcelain's age.

Oh, the stories this bowl could tell.

"Bree! Stop daydreamin' and get scrubbin'." Frankie's sharp tone cut through my thoughts before the bathroom door swung shut again—the source of the bang.

I swear, scaring me had become her life's passion. She'd picked it up from Marissa, and the two of them together were relentless.

"Stop peeking at me in the bathroom," I called out loud enough that I knew she could hear. "It's creepy."

The door opened, and my boss strode back in, her faded black boots thumping against the tile floor. As she leaned against the wall with her arms crossed, a look of amusement pulled at her thin lips and crinkled the skin around her brown eyes.

She'd been a looker back in the day, with her mess of wild curls and hipster fashion sense. Sure, plenty of people still considered the fae woman good-looking even with the thick sprouts of white hair and lines across her face, but she'd given up dating long ago.

The gym was her one true love, and no one else could compare.

"The gym's closed for lunch," she said.

"Oh, thank sweet baby Jesus." I sat back on my heels and winced as my ankle cracked against the tile. "Ow."

"Never thought you'd sound just like the rest of us landlubbers." Frankie's chuckle echoed in the tiled room as she pivoted on her heel to leave. "Finish up and come eat. I got subs."

"Because eating after scrubbing sticky crap off the toilet bowl is just *so* appetizing," I grumbled at her retreating back.

The door swung shut, leaving me alone to finish scrubbing said crap.

I sighed. Marissa was supposed to be the one cleaning today, but as usual, she'd talked her way out of it late last night. I'd hold her to her promised cleanings, no matter how long it took. She could be ninety-nine years old and wheelchair-bound, for all I cared. I'd still make her fulfill her promises.

Leaning forward again, I squeezed the spray bottle's handle, soaking the bowl in commercial-grade bleach. Scrubbing toilets to make a living hadn't been on my life's to-do list. Then again, I'd never planned on running away from home, either.

At least now we were free to do what we pleased, even if it meant living paycheck to paycheck.

Meeting the Red Dragon yesterday might have been one of the highlights of my life. Or of recent years, anyway, even if he was a cocky flirt who hadn't given me the time of day all those years ago.

Memories of Dominic's hardened muscles flexing beneath my hands rushed through me like a crashing wave. His body was so much more amazing up close than from outside the ring. Ridiculously so. No one needed to be that good-looking *and* that rich.

My attraction to him made perfect sense, and I was sure it was completely normal for any straight woman to have. Actually, any person period. Didn't mean I needed to go acting on that attraction. I bit my lip against a sudden surge of desire.

But what was one steamy night in the grand scheme of things?

As if he were even remotely interested in that prospect with a girl like me. Yes, he'd asked me out, but I was sure it was him just having some fun. He could get any woman he wanted whenever he wanted, a fact I'd seen with my own eyes on several occasions.

As far as he was concerned, I was a nobody. Just a very bad masseuse in training.

Laughing to myself, I swiped the sponge over the toilet and called it a day. No amount of scrubbing would ever make these things look clean again, but at least I'd vanquished the germs.

I winced as I stood, stretching out my sore back and legs. Thirty was a few years away and already I felt like an old blobfish. I shuddered to think how much worse I'd feel by then.

After shoving the caddy into the overpacked supply closet and thoroughly scrubbing my hands despite wearing elbow-length gloves while cleaning, I skipped down the basement steps to grab Finley.

As I approached his aquarium, the axolotl blinked sleepily up at me between gently waving strands of seaweed. He was enjoying a nap, one of many throughout the day and something I wished I had more time for.

"Hey, buddy. Sorry to wake you, but Frankie brought lunch." I submerged my arm and reached my palm toward him.

Yawning, he let out a stream of bubbles and stretched, taking his time.

"I smelled tuna," I added.

Immediately, Finley's iridescent skin swirled with color, and he swam onto my palm. He raced up my arm to perch on my shoulder, where he yipped with excitement. Unlike human-world axolotls, his kind were more than capable of making sounds whenever they wished. He could also use his magic to dry himself in a flash so as not to soak my shirt.

I laughed and dried off my arm before heading back upstairs. "You and me both."

Because luminara axolotls were even rarer on land than my kind, outings for him were few and far between. We took advantage any time the gym was closed and no one but Frankie, Marissa, or me would see him.

In Frankie's office, the promised food lay waiting on her desk, making my mouth water. It was the perfect way to recharge after a busy morning cleaning. My boss didn't glance up from her computer, and I knew better than to interrupt her.

I grabbed half of the tuna sub and sank into one of the worn chairs, hoping today wouldn't be the day the seat gave out. It held firm, and I bit into the sandwich with gusto before tearing off a chunk for Finley.

The axolotl scurried down my shoulder to the desk where I set his food. He dug in as fast as I did, and his opalescent scales shimmered brightly with happiness.

After a final mutter at her screen, Frankie leaned back in her squeaking chair and nodded to the little creature. "Heya, Fin. What's shakin'?"

Without lifting his head from the tuna, the axolotl shook his tail in response.

She cackled. "Never gets old. What a trooper."

My mouth was too full to respond, but I managed an agreeable nod.

"Look, I gotta talk to you about somethin' important." Frankie removed her reading glasses and rubbed at the bridge of her nose.

I swallowed the bite I was chewing, a bad feeling rising in my stomach. "Okay…"

She tapped some papers on her desk. They were crumpled around the edges as if picked up too many times to count. It wasn't an unusual state of affairs for paperwork in here. "The gym's in a bit of a pickle."

I drew my eyebrows together. "A what?"

"Pickle."

Was she losing her mind? I'd never heard of a pickle that large before. "How is that physically possible?"

She shot me a look like she was wondering if I'd lost my mind, too. "Ten years on land and you haven't heard that phrase? Bein' in a pickle means bein' in trouble, in a tough spot, 'tween a rock and a hard place."

I still didn't get it. "Why would anyone think a pickle means trouble?"

"Forget the pickle. The gym's in some hot water." She paused, grimaced, then threw her hands up. "Ack, damnit! The gym's in trouble, Bree."

A dollop of tuna landed on my finger. I licked it off. "You could have just said that, you know."

Gripping the edges of the desk, Frankie stared at me, her brown irises becoming tinged with violet. The fae woman was about to lose her mind.

That was what she got for using human sayings with a siren, especially one like me. "What kind of trouble?"

The violet hue faded back to brown. Crisis averted.

"Financial."

Just kidding. Crisis reinstated and lunch officially ruined.

My stomach dropped into a churning abyss. I set the rest of

my sub on the table, and Frankie shot me a sympathetic look. Money problems weren't something I could fix.

I licked my suddenly dry lips. "Do Riss and I need to move out?"

"What? No." Frankie shook her head so hard a few curls sprung loose from the pencil holding the rest back. Her idea of a makeshift hair clip. "Not yet, anyway. I'm hopin' not ever. Unless it's by choice."

I nodded slowly, not convinced. Frankie and the gym had been in one kind of debt or another since the day Marissa and I showed up in D.C., soaking wet and starving. Money issues had never been a secret between us, but she'd never had to involve me before.

If she was bringing it up now, things were bad. Bad as in Marissa and I could end up homeless again.

"I only have so much in savings, but I can—"

Frankie held up a hand. "I'm not askin' for your money."

I frowned, not sure where she was going with this. There was no way she'd ask me to do something drastic like become a stripper.

She eyed me as if expecting a certain reaction, I just didn't know what reaction she expected. "I want you to fight."

My eyes widened. Well, she'd just proved me wrong—she was going with drastic.

"I know you're about to object, but hear me out." Frankie leaned forward, placing her forearms on the desk and clasping her hands together. "No one has seen someone like you do... what you do."

She waved a hand in the air to demonstrate my magic. At least, I assumed that's what she meant by that gesture. "Your abilities would bring in a huge crowd, guaranteed. We'd have this place out of debt within a week."

My heart pounded painfully against my ribs, and my lungs burned as if the air had been sucked from the room. There was no way I could do what she was asking. That kind of visibility would draw eyes, prying eyes that could unveil our secret and expose us to my father's relentless pursuit, bringing him straight to our doorsteps.

I was paranoid enough already.

My father, a sea king driven by tradition and ambition, had sought to marry my sister and me off to other kingdoms. I vowed to protect us both from that fate, and it would all be for nothing if he found us. The possible consequences of the attention Frankie's suggestion would bring were too dire to ignore.

For the last ten years, she had been our savior, the one who took us in when we had nowhere else to go. I owed her my gratitude, my loyalty. Maybe even my life. But the path she was suggesting, this so-called solution to our financial woes, sent a chill down my spine.

After everything we'd gone through together, there was nothing I wouldn't do for her.

Except this.

Frankie must have seen the hesitation on my face. "Listen, kiddo, I wouldn't ask if I wasn't desperate. You know that, right?"

I nodded and swallowed the growing lump in my throat. "And I would do it if I could, honestly. But it's...complicated."

After a long pause, Frankie leaned back in her chair and kicked her boots up on the desk. Her expression and body language said she was unfazed, but there was no hiding the hurt and disappointment in her eyes. "Okay, sure, kid. Forget I asked. I'll figure somethin' else out. I always do."

"Frankie, it's just—" I paused and sucked in a deep breath, "I haven't been completely honest with you about...about our past."

"You think after all these years I haven't realized that?" One of her eyebrows rose. "Everyone's got secrets, kid. You wanna tell me yours, that's up to you."

I folded a corner of the sub's wrapper over, fidgeting with the crinkling paper as I worked up my courage. I could tell her more of the truth without telling her the whole truth. "Rissa and I aren't exactly orphans like we said."

Frankie chuckled and reached for an apple. "Runaways, huh? I figured it was somethin' like that."

I nodded. "Our father is, uh, controlling. To the extreme. It wasn't a good environment for either of us."

Her intense brown gaze considered me for a moment. "So, what? You worried he'll find you here if you fight?" She bit into the apple with a loud crunch.

I blinked. Geez, she was good. "Yes, exactly."

"I get that," she said between chews. "My own pops was a real asshole, beat me senseless any chance he got. But you're adults now. He can't touch you."

Except our father most definitely could. A princess's life was never her own. "Age doesn't matter in my family."

Finished with his meal—or at least as much as he could fit into his tiny stomach—Finley waddled over to the edge of the desk. He blinked his pale blue eyes until I offered him my palm, which he used to climb my arm to my shoulder. Tucking his tail around my neck, he curled up and yawned.

Frankie bit into the apple with another crunch and juice

ran down her chin. She swiped her forearm across her chin. "I can protect you. Both of you, you know that, especially once this debt is paid off. We got friends in low places." She winked.

I couldn't help but smile. That we did. The type of fighting we did here was outlawed for a reason—no rules other than to keep it in the ring. Oh, and try not to kill each other, though accidents did happen.

Frankie might be able to keep us from ending up in jail, but unfortunately, she couldn't protect us from our father. No one could.

My stomach rumbled as hunger returned with a vengeance.

Frankie nudged the tuna sub back toward me. "Fine. No fight. I need your brains then."

Picking up the sandwich, I drew my eyebrows together in confusion. Surely, she couldn't mean...

She groaned at the look on my face. "Not literally, you nerd. First the pickle, now the brain. Lord, help me. I need your help comin' up with some ideas. Fundraisers, that sorta thing."

Oh. Duh. That made way more sense than a lobotomy.

"What if we held a charity auction?" I suggested, trying to think outside the shell. "We could ask local businesses to donate items or services and then sell them off to the highest bidder."

Frankie shook her head. "Tried that a few years back, remember? It didn't bring in nearly enough money. Also, it ended up causin' trouble when some of the hot-headed bidders didn't win the items they wanted."

"Right, bad idea." I crossed it off my mental list and took a bite of my sandwich, chewing as I thought. "How about hosting a talent show? People could pay to enter, and the audience would vote for their favorite act with donations."

"Too many permits and too much organization needed for that," she said, her voice heavy with skepticism.

My phone buzzed, and I glanced at the screen. Marissa sent a text to say she had a makeup class in the evening, so she couldn't clean for me today either. I groaned.

Yet again, she was getting away with not living up to her side of the bargain. She knew she could hold her classes over my head, at least until school was over and she officially had her massage therapy license.

"Marissa may be better at this brainstorming thing than I am, she—" I paused as an idea came to me. An amazing idea that would make an evil genius proud. "Actually, Marissa would be perfect."

"You mean if she were ever here long enough to ask for ideas. I suppose kids her age just chat on one of their electronic dohickeys, right?" She barked out a laugh. "Listen to me. Do I sound old or what?" Her face sobered. "I didn't use to be this old, Gabs."

She was the only person in this world I would let call me that. Ever. Anyone else would feel my wrath via a book thrown at their head. A big, heavy, hardcover one, too.

"I meant I have an idea that might just save the gym." I took another bite of the tuna, chewing and swallowing quickly as my excitement built. "What if we offered massages to fighters and members right here in the gym? We could raise funds without drawing too much attention to ourselves, and Marissa could be the masseuse as payback for not cleaning like she said she would."

The more I thought about this idea, the more I liked it. If it was successful enough, it could turn into a long-term way of generating extra income for Subliminal. I'd keep that tidbit to myself for now, just in case it wasn't successful. No sense in getting both our hopes up.

"Since when did you become so devious?" Frankie arched a brow, amused skepticism etched into her weathered features. "You think people would pay for massages in a place like this? We're not exactly set up for a relaxin' experience."

"Oh, it'll work," I said eagerly. "We can create posters and flyers to advertise the service, and even offer discounts or package deals to attract new clients outside of gym members. It'll help pay off the debt, and I'm sure word of mouth will spread quickly."

Frankie stared at the wall, her eyes unfocused as she considered the idea. "It's unconventional, but I guess it could work. We'd need to invest in some basic supplies and equipment though. I'm not sure if we can manage it, especially with the current debt."

"That's the best part. The upfront costs would be minimal." I grinned. "We have most of the essentials already thanks to Marissa's schooling. Give me a week to get everything up and running. If it's not generating enough interest by then, we can reevaluate. But I think this can be the solution we need."

I could see the idea rolling around in Frankie's head like waves breaking against a beach, her initial doubts fading into cautious optimism. She knew how much the gym meant to me and how hard I would work to make this succeed.

Finally, she nodded and a smirk crept over her face. "Alright, let's give this a shot. But you're in charge of breakin' the news to your sister."

Relief washed over me as I realized we had found a solution that wouldn't put any of us at risk. "Deal. Knowing Rissa, she'll find a way to enjoy it."

Frankie chuckled, a glint of humor in her eyes. "Good luck, kid. You're gonna need it."

The gym was my home, these people my family. Failure wasn't an option. I would make sure this massage business became a success, no matter what. We would find a way.

We always did.

CHAPTER 8

Dominic

Dominic dodged the punch aimed at his jaw, but his reflexes were a split second too slow. As his head whipped sideways from the force of Aaron's fist, he knew he was in trouble. He ducked beneath the follow-up right hook and danced out of reach.

That was the second hit one of his friends had gotten in during their morning training session when he was usually untouchable. The Sato family's building downtown boasted a spacious private training facility. Their combined grunts and heavy breathing echoed across the vast space.

Almost every day for as long as he could remember, Dominic and his three closest and most loyal friends—Aaron, Rin, and Keiko—met to practice. Each would take a turn fighting off the other three. And for equally as long, no one had bested Dominic.

Until now.

Possibly.

Aaron's feral grin stretched ear to ear, his blue eyes bright from the exertion. "You got it bad if I was able to get a terrible swing like that in." He dipped under Dominic's swing with cat-like reflexes courtesy of his leopard shifter blood.

"Got it bad" was a gross understatement.

Less than a day had passed and Dominic's pulse still thrummed with the memory of Marissa's hands gliding over his skin. Her coy smiles and soothing touch had played on a loop in his mind since that encounter, haunting the periphery of his consciousness.

"Yeah, Nic, what's got you all spaced out?" Rin asked, easily dodging a sloppy punch. "You're off your game today."

As one of his distant cousins, Rin's dragon was also a fire elemental. The entire Sato family boasted fire spirits, the most fierce and deadly of all the elements when it came to dragons.

Dominic was certain Ichiro would have refused his bastard grandson's spirit-bonding ceremony if he hadn't proven such a valuable asset in the ring before he'd turned eighteen. The old man had wanted to see what he could do with a dragon on his side.

Little did his grandfather know at the time, the spirit of Joubunaryūō—one of the strongest Dragon Kings of old— would choose Dominic. Ichiro never would have allowed it had he known.

"More like what's her name?" Keiko's teasing voice asked from behind him.

He shook off the memories clouding his mind and focused on the fight, lashing out with a series of quick jabs and kicks.

Nimble as ever, Keiko and Rin darted out of reach and shared a knowing grin. Those two had been lovebirds from the moment they first set eyes on each other in middle school. It was as unlikely a pairing as Dominic's parents, but no one outside this small group knew about the relationship.

Both had black hair and dark eyes, but their similarities ended there. While Rin's beast-like, bodybuilder's form made him look like he could eat an entire cow for dinner and still be hungry, Keiko was pint-sized and a smattering of freckles danced across her otherwise pale nose.

She was the perfect example of size not mattering. Her naturally lethal skills and abilities were unique, which was why Ichiro adopted her fifteen years ago, and she had become like a little sister to Dominic. Unrelated to the Satos by blood, yet more accepted by the family than he would ever be.

Regardless, he wasn't like the rest of them. He didn't fall for anyone. He couldn't.

Not yet.

He didn't have time for the kind of distraction Marissa posed, not when his position within his family's empire was at stake. Securing his place as heir was paramount for his plan to succeed, and chasing after a woman would only slow him down.

With a growl, Dominic allowed the simmering beast within him to rise. Letting his dragon loose was far too dangerous in his current state of mind, but scaring them would go a long way to easing his frustration.

Keiko took a step back, narrowing her eyes. She'd been on the receiving end of his dragon's wrath before. "You wouldn't."

"Wouldn't I?" He kept his voice low and dangerous.

This time, Aaron rolled his eyes and stood straight, sweat dripping down his tan cheeks. "Admit it, Dominic. She's got you whipped over a fucking massage. And it wasn't even a rub and tug."

"This's about that masseuse? The one I met at your place yesterday?" Rin's eyes widened, and then he nodded. "She was a fox."

Had it been anyone else making a comment like that about Marissa, Dominic might have felt threatened enough to attack. Instead, he dropped his arms in defeat.

His friends were right. He was completely distracted by that brown-haired beauty. More of an auburn with those streaks of red that glittered like gold in the light. He'd never thought of a woman's hair like that before, hardly gave the color more than a cursory glance.

But Marissa was different.

Everything about her was different, unique, seductive. Her essence called to him at all hours, day and night, and it had only been a day. No, not even twenty-four hours.

He found himself wondering what kind of shampoo she used, and how she took her coffee. All the little details that made up a person. A vivid fantasy of her laughing over breakfast in little more than one of his t-shirts flashed through his mind, and he shook his head to dispel it.

"Fine, I admit it," Dominic said and shrugged it off. "But it'll pass, like all the others."

Rin headed to the side benches and grabbed a bottle of water. "Bullshit it's like all the others. We're not blind. Want me to run a background check?"

Brushing wet strands of hair back from his face, Dominic followed. Aaron and Keiko were hot on his heels. "No, I've got this handled."

He leaned against the wall, trying to slow his pulse and clear his mind. But unwanted thoughts of Marissa persisted, haunting him. She was like a drug, and he was an addict after just one hit.

Keiko sidled up next to him with a knowing smirk. "So again, what's her name?"

He cast her a withering glare. "There is no her because it's not happening."

"Yeah, and I'm the tooth fairy." Aaron stretched his arms behind his back in a languid manner. "Come on, we've known you for most of our lives. Who is she?"

"Megan?" Rin rubbed his chin thoughtfully. "Melissa?"

"Marissa, and this conversation is over. She wasn't interested."

Aaron laughed. "So that's what's got you all twisted up, huh? The great Dominic Sato shot down at last."

Irritation flared, but beneath it, a traitorous part of him couldn't deny the truth in Aaron's words. The masseuse had caught him off guard in a way no woman ever had. And that both thrilled and unsettled him.

"Since when has that stopped you from getting what you wanted?" Keiko crossed her arms and cocked her hip to the side. "She won't say no forever, if only to say she went on a date with a Sato."

Dominic shook his head. He knew Marissa was different. She would have been a challenge, a thought that excited him, but now was not the time.

"Seriously, Nic, we want to see you happy for once." Keiko's voice had taken on a soft tone, and he met her gaze. "You deserve happiness."

"I can't afford to think about happiness," Dominic shot back, his voice tense as he conveyed his hidden meaning. "Not when I'm so close."

Although they were alone in the training facility, he knew cameras and hidden microphones were as abundant here as in Dominic's penthouse, except there they were all his. The old man wasn't any more paranoid than any other ruler sitting on a precarious throne.

Still, they kept any discussions about their plans with Ichiro to more secure locations. Even discussing Marissa at all felt like a risk. If his grandfather knew Dominic had a weakness, Ichiro wouldn't hesitate to use her against him.

"Who says you can't do both?" Rin countered. "Maybe this is exactly what you need—someone who challenges you, makes you question things, and ultimately makes you stronger."

"Is she Gifted?" Keiko asked. After he nodded, she said, "Good, that'll make things easier."

Exhaustion clung to Dominic like a second skin, but beneath the fatigue was a restless energy he couldn't shake. His friends' words echoed in his mind, their persuasion wearing away at his resistance. Maybe they were right.

He knew he should focus on the impossible—gaining Ichiro's favor. Pursuing a woman, no matter how intriguing, was trouble waiting to happen. Once he took over the empire and made some massive changes to the way business was run, then he could focus on his own happiness.

Except curiosity burned hot and bright within him, ignited by Marissa's mysterious hold over him. He wanted to see her again, to uncover the secrets behind her quirky smile and guarded eyes.

Rin tossed Dominic a towel. "We're going out for lunch. You in?"

Wiping the sweat from his neck, Dominic shook his head. "Not today."

"Ah, so the mighty Red Dragon has given in at last," Keiko teased. "Planning to see a certain, uninterested masseuse?"

Dominic opened his mouth to object, but no argument

came. The human side of him wanted to rip something to shreds in frustration, but Jou purred in contentment. The beast wanted nothing more than to take what he thought was his, which was this woman who'd enchanted them both.

His friends were right—he couldn't deny his feelings any longer. Besides, he had never been one to back down from a challenge, and Marissa was a mystery he was determined to solve.

Perhaps once he did, this infatuation would pass.

With a wry smile, he raised his hands in surrender. "Okay, okay. I have a lunch meeting with a potential client, but I'll track her down after."

His friends erupted into laughing cheers, slapping him on the back and offering enthusiastic encouragement. Dominic allowed himself a moment to enjoy it, anticipation building within him.

This pursuit would be anything but ordinary. Just from one meeting, he knew Marissa wasn't like other women. If he wanted to win her over, he would have to approach this strategically. No more careless flirtation or hollow charm.

She deserved more than that, and he found, possibly for the first time when it came to a woman, that he wanted to give her more.

Later today, he would visit the massage school. Only this time, he wouldn't be dissuaded so easily. He had made up his mind, and once Dominic Sato set his sights on something, he didn't give up until it was his.

CHAPTER 9

Dominic

Three hours later, Dominic stood outside the front doors of the massage school, not far from the Foggy Bottom Metro station. Cars zipped by, splashing through puddles left by the morning rain, while pedestrians navigated the crowded sidewalks.

The school took up a narrow, three-story brick building wedged between a nail salon and a coffee shop. Visible through the large front windows, a reception desk and several closed doors led to private massage rooms.

His heart thrummed in anticipation. When was the last time he'd felt this nervous about asking a woman on a date? Years, at least, if ever. Getting women had never been a problem—his charm, good looks, and reputation usually did all the work.

Taking a deep, steadying breath, Dominic opened the door and stepped into the lobby. Immediately, the scent of lavender and eucalyptus curled around him, soothing his heightened senses. Soft instrumental music played in the background and created a serene atmosphere that contrasted sharply with the chaos outside.

He approached the reception desk, smiling as the young blonde woman sitting behind it looked up. "Good afternoon. I'm here to see Marissa Johnson."

Taking in the flowers he held, her eyes widened. "Marissa? Sure. Just a moment." She picked up the phone and dialed a number. Her cheeks flushed a delicate pink as she snuck a glance at him again. "Hey, you have a visitor."

Knowing Marissa would be there that day because he'd called ahead to ask, Dominic arrived with a bouquet of red roses and had dressed in a pair of expensive yet comfortable dark jeans and a button-down shirt. He had considered asking her out to dinner over the phone, but the more he thought about it, the more he realized asking her in person would be better.

She wouldn't be able to resist his charm so easily, and his presence would show his sincerity.

A moment later, a petite yet curvy young woman with red hair and bright blue eyes entered the lobby from within the school. There was something familiar about her face and the way she moved, though Dominic was sure he'd never seen her before.

Even though they weren't medical professionals, every student wore a matching set of scrubs with the school's logo embroidered on the front, just as Marissa had done the day before. The new woman took one glance at Dominic and her jaw went slack.

He flashed one of his best smiles, knowing how devastating it could be. Maybe winning Marissa's peers over would work in his favor.

Snapping her mouth shut, the woman glanced at the receptionist, who nodded at Dominic. Confusion made his smile falter as the red-headed woman approached him. Her lips transformed into a gorgeous smile.

"May I help you?" Her voice was light and lyrical, the opposite of Marissa's more sultry timbre.

"No, thank you," he said. "I'm waiting for someone."

Her smile twisted into a cute smirk. "Me, I presume. I'm Marissa Johnson. You asked to see me?"

Now it was his turn for his mouth to go slack. There must have been a mistake. "You're Marissa?"

She took a step closer and touched his arm. "Don't look so disappointed, Mr...?"

Despite his confusion, Dominic recovered quickly. "Sato. Dominic Sato."

Her blue eyes flew open wide, and she glanced at the receptionist, who was pretending not to eavesdrop. Poorly, he noted.

The red-haired woman claiming to be Marissa waved him farther away from the desk, her cheeks turning almost the same shade as her hair. "Please don't be upset, Mr. Sato. I can explain."

He raised his eyebrows. "I'm more confused than anything."

She took a deep breath. "My sister is the one who gave you your massage yesterday. I was caught out in Virginia and wouldn't make it back in time for your appointment. You know how D.C. traffic is." She waved her hand toward the door leading out. "Bree's always been quick to pick up new skills, and she owed me."

Bree.

The name washed over him with a soothing sensation, like finding solace on land after being lost at sea. Dominic replayed the massage in his head, remembering how he'd wondered just how new she'd been.

So new, she didn't go to this school.

As he studied the real Marissa's face, the family resemblance was unmistakable. Her hair was more red than Bree's and her eyes more blue than seafoam, but full lips and a slight dimple in her chin matched Bree's exactly. Not to mention skin so white it was almost translucent.

"I'd be more than happy to schedule a make-up appointment, on the house." She pressed her hands together in a plea. "Just *please* keep this between us." Her gaze dipped to the bouquet he held, and she smiled. "Are those for me?"

He huffed out a laugh. "Yes and no."

"I'd apologize," her smile morphed into a cunning look, "but it seems like the massage went well?"

"Very well. Where can I find Bree?" Saying her name aloud stiffened his cock to half-mast.

Marissa narrowed her eyes, her smile gone. "How do I know you're not a killer?"

Well, that was a tricky question. He *was* a killer. "I'm not going to kill your sister."

"That's what a killer would say." She crossed her arms.

"Are you always this stubborn?"

"Do you always bring your masseuse flowers?"

Dominic stared at this tiny creature who showed no fear of talking to him this way. Her sister was either extremely fortunate or extremely unlucky. He had a feeling it was both.

She relaxed her arms. "I'm a little protective, you know?"

"No judgment. I would like to ask your sister out to dinner." He raised the bouquet and winked. "In person, preferably."

Marissa's smile returned. "Just promise you're not going to kill her. Or stalk her, Or maim her. Or—"

"I won't do anything she doesn't want me to do."

Unless she begs me to, he thought, imagining an intimate scenario involving handcuffs.

She nodded, satisfied. "She's at Subliminal."

Confusion laced his thoughts again. "The gym? She trains there?"

"Oh gods, no. She's... Well, you'll see." She glanced down at her watch. "I gotta get back before they come looking for me. Good luck!"

Twirling on her toes, Marissa was gone before Dominic had a chance to process the last part of their conversation.

He would see?

What the hell did that mean?

♪ ♫ ♩ ♫ ♪

DOMINIC STARED AT THE DOOR LEADING INTO THE gym where he'd spent over a decade spilling his blood, sweat, and tears until he was the best. Dread churned in his stomach like undigested rotten food.

This was the last place he wanted to come back to, and if he had his way with the family empire, he never would again. Not to fight, at any rate.

The gym sat between two other buildings on a busy downtown street near Judiciary Square. To non-Gifted humans, it was a nondescript building that drew little notice. They ignored it as they passed, even if someone were to open the door right in front of them. The non-Gifted would simply sidestep around the door and keep going their merry way.

In addition to using her fae magic—evident in the triskelion, a symbol with three spirals swirling out from a central point, etched above the door—Frankie Delgado had paid a small fortune to the Sato family for a camouflaging charm they'd procured. Both magics had done their job well disguising the building for over twenty-five years.

Luckily for Frankie, the charm would continue to work forever so long as the stone stayed intact, which is one reason why no one had seen it since. Dominic wouldn't have put it past her to bury the damn thing in the foundation.

The Gifted Interests Government had tried for years to infiltrate the gym during a fight night, intending to shut it down for good. But Frankie must have gotten her grubby fae hands on another charm that kept them away as well. That, or she had someone on the inside, which was the more likely scenario.

No one knew exactly how she'd evaded the agents for so long, but the Gifted who frequented the fights continued to line their pockets while her luck—or magic—held firm. However, it would take far more than any charms she could procure to keep someone as powerful as Dominic out.

He took a deep breath and pulled open the door, stepping inside. As his eyes adjusted to the dimmer interior, a soft humming drifted from the opposite side of the main ring. He was about to announce his presence when the most beautiful sound in the world stopped him in his tracks.

A woman's voice, sweeter than any angel's, belted out an old jazz tune he hadn't heard in years. It was a classic by Ella Fitzgerald, and he was utterly captivated.

"It looks as if we two will never be one..."

Entranced, Dominic stepped forward. He had to know who

was singing, who ensnared him with such a magnificent sound. As he moved around the boxing ring, he slowed, drinking in the sight of the woman before him. His heart beat faster.

It was her—*Bree*.

She held a mop in both hands and swept it over the cement floor in time with the song's tune. Her moves were beautiful and elegant, a dance of pure joy.

"*Something must be done...*"

Cute but worn running shorts and a matching sports bra did little to cover her toned body. She was barefoot, and a ponytail held most of her hair back from her face, all except the unruliest of them all.

Bree paused to lift the mop into the bucket, then pushed some escaped strands of hair behind her ear. Her gaze lifted to his, and she gasped.

CHAPTER 10

Bree

Frozen in place, I stared at Dominic Sato as if I were seeing a ghost. My jaw—and ability to function in general—went slack.

Oh, for the love of Tethys.

The mop handle slipped out of my grip and sailed toward the ground. I lunged to grab it, afraid it would tip the entire yellow bucket over, only to trip over the bucket myself. I wind-milled my arms as if they would somehow transform into wings and keep me from falling on my ass.

Especially in front of the hottest man to ever exist on this planet.

But instead of hitting the ground, a strong hand grabbed me beneath the arm and hauled me back onto my feet. Dominic's foot shot out and caught the rocking bucket's lip, keeping it from tipping over. Only a small amount of water sloshed over the side as the bucket settled.

Yeesh. His reflexes were insanely fast.

We stood there for a moment with his hand holding my arm, our bodies pressed together, my heart racing. Unlike during the massage, he didn't smell like the oils I kneaded into his skin.

Today, he smelled like a campfire, a smoky, slightly spicy scent that was similar to sandalwood but wasn't quite the same. He smelled absolutely delicious.

As our eyes locked, a spark passed between us.

Or maybe it was static.

Either way, my panic returned in a rush.

Oh coconuts, he was here. The last time I'd seen the man, my last word had been, "Toodles." *Toodles*, for flounder's sake. As if that weren't embarrassing enough, now I had to see his stupidly handsome face again.

Shaking my head to break the spell his gaze had over me, I stepped away and he released my arm. "What are you doing here?"

Real smooth, Bree.

"Marissa told me where to find you." He bent to pick up the mop and placed it back in the bucket's holder before grinning at me. "The real Marissa, I should add. She mentioned something about you stepping in for her because you owed her."

"What!" My mouth dropped open again. Leave it to Marissa to turn things around like that. "That lying little... She owes *me*. Never the other way around."

My exasperation only seemed to amuse Dominic further. "After meeting her, I can believe that."

I sighed. "Well, on behalf of us both, I apologize. I'm not in the habit of impersonating my sister, in case you were wondering."

He chuckled. "Duly noted. Though I can't say I object to the results."

I wasn't sure what results he referred to, but I also hadn't noticed the bouquet of red roses in his hand until just then. Not a single petal or leaf had fallen during his rescue of my clumsy near-fall.

The romantic gesture was surprising for someone like him but also had me rolling my eyes internally. Roses. Pretty, but typical. "Stopped by before a date?"

"That's the plan." Delight twinkled across his whiskey-hued eyes.

The thought of him taking another woman on a date made a knot twist in my stomach. Which was just ridiculous. My little fantasy of a steamy night together was just that—a fantasy. "Don't want to keep her waiting. Did you need something else?"

"I need you to answer a question first," he said.

I raised an eyebrow. "Go for it."

"I'd like to take you to dinner."

I blinked at him. Wait, what? He wanted to take *me* out? Like, for real? I must be high on bleach fumes or still daydreaming back in the bathroom. This couldn't be real life.

For one, I looked and smelled atrocious. He had gotten an up-close-and-personal whiff when he caught me.

For two, he was way out of my league. Fathoms. Whatever was deeper than fathoms, that far. There was no way he actually wanted to take me on a date knowing what he did now.

The silence stretched on until he finally asked, "Well?"

I shifted my weight slightly. "Well, what?"

"You didn't answer my question."

"Technically, you didn't ask a question," I pointed out and immediately grimaced.

Was everyone this awkward around impossibly good-looking men?

Or just me?

He grinned. "I sense a family resemblance in more than looks. Are you always this difficult?"

"Yes, now go away. The gym's closed for cleaning." Mentally kicking myself for not locking the door earlier, I reached for the mop and bucket, ready to get back to work. With any luck, he'd take the hint.

"Can I take you to dinner?"

Today was not my lucky day. "I mean, you *can* because you're physically able to. But you *may* not. Scram."

Spinning away from him, I pushed the bucket in front of me. My face practically caught on fire, and my heartbeat thudded loudly in my ears. I didn't think I could get any more awkward, yet here I was, spouting off grammar rules and words like "scram."

"Give me a chance, Bree. One dinner."

This man was persistent. I blew out an exasperated breath, refusing to face him again. I'd give in if I did. "This is ridiculous. You don't even know me. Why in the world would you want to take *me* to dinner?"

"Because I know you've got an interesting story to tell," he said softly against my ear, his breath raising goosebumps across my skin. I hadn't even heard him move. "And I want to hear it."

Shrugging to hide a shiver, I ducked away from him and finally met his gaze. "Sorry to disappoint you, but I'm just a janitor. Nothing interesting to see here."

"That's not what I see at all." He studied me intently, heat rising within me wherever his gaze fell. "You move like a skilled fighter. Graceful, alert, balanced. And those scars across your knuckles suggest you've thrown more than a punch or two."

I froze, my heart pounding almost painfully against my ribs. His ability to read me that easily after so little time together filled me with fear.

Who else might have realized I was hiding something?

I needed to get away from him. Far, far away.

But before I had a chance to escape, Frankie walked out of her office and bumped into me. She had a stack of paperwork in her hands, flipping through them with a look of confusion. She hadn't noticed our intruder yet.

"Oh, good, you're—" Her words cut off when she finally looked up, peering at me over the ridge of her pink glasses. Her gaze narrowed as it landed on Dominic, and she straightened her back. "Dominic Sato. What in the Otherworld are you doin' here?"

Exactly what I'd asked and now wished I hadn't.

Frankie knowing who he was didn't surprise me. She made it a point to stay up-to-date on the who's who of the Gifted community, if only to know who to bribe and when to keep this place off the radar.

I did the opposite. Getting caught up in something like a forbidden romance novel was much more satisfying than trying to keep up with the latest gossip.

To his credit, Dominic smiled. "Just keeping our favorite janitor company. Always a pleasure to see you, Frankie."

She snorted and crossed her arms, unconcerned with the papers she crumpled beneath her armpit as she did so. "You call me Frankie one more time like we're buddies and I'll be sure you never step foot in here again."

Despite the threat, his smile only widened, and he pressed a hand over his heart. "You wound me. Surely after all this time you consider me a friend."

Frankie muttered something under her breath that sounded suspiciously like making dragon stew. "What d'ya want, dragon?"

Dominic raised the bouquet of roses and nodded toward me. "I'm wooing your girl here. Trying to, anyway. She's playing hard to get."

I glared at him and considered tipping the bucket of dirty water over, aiming for his expensive shoes. Almost, but I couldn't bring myself to do it since I'd be the one mopping it all up. "I'm not playing anything. I said no, move on."

Frankie's expression changed from dark suspicion to pure, wide-eyed amazement. She pushed her reading glasses into her mess of curly hair and blinked slowly. "You turned down Dominic Sato? A dragon? The *Red* Dragon?"

Considering how long he'd fought at her gym and she organized all the fights, it wasn't a complete surprise that she knew he was also the Red Dragon. I was mildly miffed she hadn't confided that juicy tidbit to me at some point over the years, but I also knew all I'd had to do was ask. Except I hadn't cared enough to know his identity before now.

"Why is this so hard for the two of you to understand?" I asked, throwing my hands up in exasperation. "I'm busy."

Frankie let out a hoot of laughter. "Too busy with your newest book boyfriend, you mean. Which one is it this week? Viking or highlander?"

My cheeks blazed with heat, and I never wanted to crawl beneath a rock more than at that moment. Usually, I didn't mind anyone knowing what I read or discussing the merits of romance. But usually, I wasn't standing in front of the hottest man on the planet, one who'd just asked me out to dinner.

How did one handle this sort of situation?

Dominic turned his grin on me, appraising me from head to foot. "Wouldn't a real-life dragon be more exciting than one in a book? I'd be happy to reenact any favorite scenes."

I closed my eyes and groaned, ready to be swallowed up by the floor. Any moment now. *Come on floor, don't let me down.* "For your information, not that it's any of your business, but he's a grim reaper, and I'm not—"

"Why don't you challenge her to a fight?" Frankie's voice cut in.

I snapped my eyes open and stared at her. She couldn't be serious.

CHAPTER 11

Bree

"What?" Dominic and I asked simultaneously.

Frankie tugged her glasses out of her hair, leaving some strands sticking up in odd directions. She chewed on one end while her gaze flicked between us as she concocted some hair-brained idea. "Yeah, this could be good. If you win, dragon boy, she's gotta agree to this date."

"See, I knew we were friends." Dominic winked at her.

"And when he loses?" I asked, hands on my hips. Not that I was entertaining this crazy idea.

His chuckle was low and seductive, teasing my nerves into a frenzy. "Oh, darlin', I never lose."

Traitorous warmth flooded through me. I quirked an eyebrow, ignoring my body's reaction to the best of my ability. "First time for everything, right? Just like a woman saying 'no'?"

He ambled toward me, slow and sure, and his intense gaze held me captive. "What do you want in the unlikely scenario I lose?"

I held my head steady as I looked into his deep amber eyes. "For you to stop harassing me."

His gaze dipped to my lips, and it was a real struggle not to lick them nervously. "Is that what you want?"

No. Yes. Maybe? I was swimming blind here. What I wanted was a fantasy, a fairytale, a figment of my imagination. I wanted the impossible, which meant what I wanted didn't matter. What I *needed* was to forget this man ever existed.

I raised my chin defiantly. "Yes."

His eyes searched mine before he gave a clipped nod. "Deal."

"Oh, this is gonna be so much fun." Frankie waved a hand toward the front door. The deadbolt sparked with a violet light and slid shut with a thunk. "Lemme get my doodad." She hurried back into her office.

"Wait here." I held up a finger to stop Dominic from closing the gap between us and rushed after Frankie. I closed her office door behind me and leaned against it. "What do you think you're doing?" I hissed.

She made a pfft noise as she rustled through a desk drawer. "Oh please, this'll be a piece of cake. You've watched him fight for years, kid. You know all his tells, and he has no idea what he's in for." She cackled.

My resolve was crumbling. "I know I just agreed, but I can't do this. I can't let anyone know what I am and definitely not *him*."

"Found it." Letting out a whoop of excitement, she held up a dull grey rock and beamed like she'd found a fabled pearl of Tethys. "You can with this."

"How is a rock going to help?"

"This little beauty is an oath-keeper," she explained. "You'll both swear to keep the details of the fight between us and neither of you will be able to discuss it with anyone else. It's like the equivalent of a magical NDA."

I furrowed my eyebrows, remembering Dominic mentioning those letters during the massage. I hadn't known what he meant, but I was sure Marissa would have so I'd played along. "A what?"

"Non-disclosure agreement. Humans love 'em, but ours are more ironclad, just without the iron."

"He'll still know about me, Frankie. What I am." A shiver ran up my spine, but I didn't know if it was from fear of him finding out or desire.

"But he won't be able to tell anyone about it. The knowledge'll be useless. Now come on." Pushing me out of the way, she pulled open the office door and headed out.

I ran a hand over my face, not quite sure how I got myself into this mess. Somehow it was all Marissa's fault. Again.

Forget three cleanings. She owed me a month.

Back in the main gym, Frankie strode purposefully toward the ring while pointing toward the supply cabinet. "Yo, dragon, grab a bucket of water and bring it over."

Amazingly, he didn't question the command. While he set the flower bouquet down on a bench and did as she asked— well, demanded—I followed after my boss, ducking beneath the ladder-style ropes and onto the ring's padded flooring.

When Dominic joined us, hefting the filled bucket and setting it down in a corner, Frankie held up the rock. "Once I activate the oath-keeper, none of us will be able to discuss this fight with anyone else. *Capiche*?"

Dominic glanced at me and nodded, a smile on his beautifully full lips. "*Capiche*."

My gaze snagged on those lips, and I couldn't help but

wonder how they'd feel pressed against mine. I realized they were both staring at me. "Got it."

Frankie shook her head. "You gotta say *capiche*."

"Why? I understand the rules."

"Godsdamn it, Bree, just say it," she said with an exasperated huff.

This was ridiculous. "Fine. *Capiche*."

The rock trembled in her hand before turning pitch black like obsidian. Rising from her palm, it lifted into the air above our heads, and a dome of shadows spread out around the ring, trapping us inside.

Oh, I guess *capiche* was the magic word to activate the spell. Would have been nice to know such details ahead of time.

"Hurry up and get ready." Frankie scurried to the side and slipped under the rope. The dome extended a few feet outside the ring, so she had room to move around without leaving the spelled area.

Dominic wasted no time. He pulled his shirt over his head and tossed it over the frame, landing right on Frankie's head.

"What the! You deadbeat dodo," her muffled voice yelled out before she could yank it off her face. "Not cool, dragon." She was about to throw the shirt on the ground but stopped and sniffed it. "Hm, nice cologne."

Not that Dominic or I were paying her much attention anymore.

My gaze was glued to those rock-hard abs and the smooth planes of his chest. Despite his toned muscles, he was long and lean and absolute perfection.

By the tide, I hadn't appreciated just how unbelievably sexy this man was during the massage.

When I finally lifted my gaze to his face, he watched me

with amusement. He kicked off his shoes, nudging them off the side, then removed his socks and jeans.

Standing there in nothing but red boxers that somehow enhanced the generous package hiding within, he looked every bit a god risen from smoldering embers. If I wasn't careful, I'd start drooling.

Smirking, Dominic rolled his shoulders. "I'll go easy on you, princess. Wouldn't want to damage that pretty face."

My heart skipped a beat until I remembered he had no idea who I really was. It was just a cute nickname. Two could play at that game. I snorted. "In your dreams, lizard boy."

As Frankie guffawed from the sidelines, his eyes flashed dangerously. The air around him shimmered with a crimson haze.

Dragon magic.

Curling my hands into fists until my nails dug into my palms, I spun on my heel and stalked over to the full water bucket. This was such a terrible idea.

And yet, I didn't want to stop either. It had been so long since I'd last used my magic, like *really* used it against an actual opponent. My palms practically itched as I grabbed the bucket and hoisted it into the air.

Before I had a chance to chicken out, I poured the bucket's contents over my head.

I gasped as ice-cold water splashed over me, dousing me from head to foot. I swiped a hand over my face and set the bucket down before turning to face Dominic.

He stared at me with wide eyes and a slack jaw, his gaze dipping to my soaking-wet top that clung to my breasts like a second skin.

Yeah... I hadn't thought that through properly.

Thankfully, there was no time to explain.

"Begin!" Frankie's voice called out.

Instantly, I released my magic from the tight hold I kept it under. As my body soaked up the water drenching my skin and clothes, the call of the sea washed over me.

I sank into the salty depths of my magic, letting the ocean tides and the moon's pull move me wherever they desired. The hair across my body rose on end as I delighted in a sensation I'd missed for far too long.

A thousand memories rushed forward next, nearly drowning me in their intensity. Of coral hallways and bubbles of laughter, of games of tag among rows of seaweed and flashing scales on mermaid tails.

As the memories swept me away, I almost missed Dominic's attack. I flung up a hastily formed water shield to block the fire spear he'd thrown.

He narrowed his eyes as the weapon doused quickly. The spear evaporated far too easily, which meant he was holding back to test me. He hadn't even released his dragon yet.

His mistake.

I might have been born a princess, but that hadn't stopped me from badgering my father to allow me to train with his soldiers. He'd finally given in when I was seven, and I hadn't looked back. I practiced with them every single day until the day I left home.

Since then, I'd spent the last ten years watching the fighters in this very ring. I'd learned so much more about my own abilities than my father ever showed me and practiced as often as I could when no one else was around. No one but Frankie.

I was confident that I was as good as any of them, maybe even better. I just never had the chance to prove it.

Until now.

With a sudden burst of speed, Dominic lunged forward, claws extended.

I sidestepped his attack, my movements flowing as gracefully as a river's current, and countered with a swift kick that landed against his midsection.

He grunted as my kick propelled him forward into the ropes. With his back to me, he glanced over his shoulder and grinned. There was a glimmer of vulnerability in his gaze, a hint of pride and passion hidden beneath his fierce exterior.

Despite the purpose of this battle, the flutter of an unexpected emotion stirred to life deep within me.

The black ink tattooed across his back glowed red. Emerging from his skin, a shimmering form slithered through the air, growing as long as Dominic was tall.

A dragon born of molten lava soared overhead and released a powerful, terror-inducing roar. The air wavered with the intense heat spewing from the beast's open maw.

My jaw went slack. I had seen the magnificent creature plenty of times before, but never this close. It was unbelievably beautiful.

Taking advantage of the distraction, Dominic seized my wrist in an attempt to immobilize me, and our eyes locked.

Time stood still.

In that electrifying moment, I felt a connection, an undeniable attraction that soared beyond our exteriors. The lines between us being adversaries and something much more intimate blurred.

Before his dragon could interfere, I twisted my body free of his grasp and delivered a punishing roundhouse kick that sent him staggering sideways.

Growling low and deep, his gaze was now a mixture of determination and something unspoken. Something primal and predatory that sent a shiver up my spine.

The airborne beast shot toward me with the speed of a flaming arrow.

With a flick of my hand, I summoned a powerful wall of water around Dominic and me, blocking the dragon from reaching its target unless it wanted to extinguish itself.

More water surged around Dominic and immobilized him in a vortex of liquid force. Leaping into the air, I kicked him squarely in his chest.

He crashed to the mat flat on his back, beaten.

Hardly breaking a sweat, I gazed down at him and smirked. "I win."

Only after saying the words did I regret them. I mean, I wanted to win, but I didn't want the prize I said I did. I didn't want him to leave me alone.

What's more, I expected him to be furious about losing. As far as I knew, he'd never lost a fight in this ring. But fury wasn't what his gaze reflected.

No, he looked downright rapturous while staring up at me.

Maybe he liked getting his ass handed to him.

"What in the seven Hells are you?" he asked, his voice hushed with awe as he sat up.

Backing away, I shook my head, not quite sure what I was saying no to. My hands and voice trembled. "Nothing. Forget this ever happened. Forget me."

His dragon rumbled over our heads, but I couldn't decipher the sound.

The dome of shadows surrounding the ring popped and

disappeared, and the oath-keeping rock dropped into the middle of the ring, lifeless once again.

My magic still swam inside me, bursting to get out. That fight had been too quick. It wasn't enough of a release, and if I didn't get out of there fast, people might die—just like my mother had. A cold sweat formed across my forehead.

Frankie's slow clap jarred me from my thoughts, and I met her knowing gaze.

Without another word, I fled from the ring.

SJ FOWLER
@NIGHT.WITCHERY

CHAPTER 12
Dominic

Sweat dripped down Dominic's face, and his chest heaved from the fight's exertion. A tsunami had swept through his body and soul, leaving him breathless and longing for more.

In a matter of minutes, his life had changed.

He stared after Bree, unable to tear his gaze away from the door through which she'd just disappeared, fleeing from the ring. His heart pounded with a mix of adrenaline and desire so intense, it blazed a path through his veins.

Her magic was unlike anything he'd encountered before. It was seductive, almost erotic, and he'd wanted to bathe in her glory rather than fight against her. She moved with an experienced fighter's grace as if she'd been training her entire life.

Yet he'd never seen someone with her magic fight or even train in this ring, and he'd made it a point to watch or keep up with most Subliminal matches over the years. There wasn't a chance in hell he'd simply missed mention of someone like her.

As his dragon spirit flowed back into his skin, it roared in frustration, an urge to chase after Bree consuming every fiber of their combined being. The disappointment of losing his first fight only served to fuel Dominic's determination to win her heart, and an unspoken understanding settled deep within that she would be his.

His chosen mate.

He wiped the sweat from his brow and took a deep, steadying breath. Silently, he promised to show Bree just how much he wanted her and the lengths he would go to prove it.

"Told you she'd wipe the floor with your sorry ass." Chuckling from the sidelines, Frankie reached beneath the rope and grabbed the oath-keeper. She tossed the grey rock into the air once then slipped it into her pocket. "Such a shame I can't convince her to fight for me, eh?"

Dominic needed to use the ropes to pull himself to his feet, the unsettling power of Bree's magic still coursing through his unsteady legs. Not to mention the bruises already forming along his jaw and ribs.

"Is she what I think she is?" No water witch he knew could wield magic like that.

The old woman clucked her tongue. "Not my secret to tell, lizard boy. Now get lost and stop pesterin' us."

Like hell he would. Straightening his back, he met her gaze with a fiery determination that burned to the depths of his soul. "The oath-keeper only stops me from discussing the fight, not from continuing to pursue Bree."

Frankie's lips quirked to the side. "Fightin' dirty, I see. A dragon is as a dragon does, I s'pose. Welp, don't say I didn't warn you." She gestured to the front door as she headed for her office. "Show yourself out."

Dominic glanced back in the direction Bree had fled. The memory of her earlier singing swirled around him. It was an enchanting melody that stirred something primal within him.

Her voice and the feelings it provoked solidified his belief that he knew what she was.

Her scent, a mixture of saltwater and jasmine, clung to him like an invisible tether that bound them together. Every cell in his body screamed at him to find her, claim her, make her understand that they were meant for each other.

However, following her wouldn't do much good at the moment. He knew wherever that door led, she was long gone from here.

No matter.

He would figure out a way to win her over, and then she would be his.

AFTER A SHOWER AND CHANGE OF CLOTHES BACK AT his Wharf penthouse, Dominic settled into his leather chair and switched on the computer. His thoughts turned to the task at hand—planning the perfect surprise date.

One date.

That was all he needed to prove he wasn't whoever she thought he was and win her over. He was sure of it. If the only way he could get her on a date was by surprise, then he'd make sure the entire night was unforgettable.

The idea of giving Bree a night filled with romance and adventure filled him with an unfamiliar eagerness. To everyone but his closest friends, Dominic was a playboy and only good for his skill in the ring. Little more than hired muscle.

Hiding the truth was the only way to keep a target off his back. He would own the Sato empire by the time anyone figured him out, and by then, he would be unstoppable.

Deceiving everyone, particularly Ichiro and Kenzo, was one of the few joys in his life.

But for Bree, he would show a side of himself that most believed he was incapable of. One that was gentle, caring, and utterly devoted to her happiness.

As he considered the patterns of their lives thus far, a smile tugged at the corners of his mouth. A janitor at Subliminal. Either fate had a sense of humor, or it was merely a cruel twist of irony that had brought them together under such unlikely circumstances.

She wasn't exactly who she was pretending to be, either. Her magic might have been unlike anything he'd personally experienced before, but he recognized the signs from his studies of various Gifted types. She was a siren, or a mermaid as humans called her kind. He'd bet his life on it.

As far as he knew, sirens didn't suddenly grow legs and walk on land. He couldn't remember the last time anyone had claimed to see a siren, on land or at all. If someone had, they kept it a secret. A closely guarded secret, since few in the Gifted population could keep secrets from someone as resourceful and wealthy as a Sato.

No, there was more to Bree's story, and he was determined to discover it all.

Regardless of who or what she truly was, he knew one thing for certain—she had awakened something within him, a fierce desire to protect and cherish her that went beyond mere attraction. He would stop at nothing to claim her as his mate.

Jou rumbled his agreement before settling in for a nap.

After jotting down his ideas in an email, Dominic called his closest friends for a virtual group meeting. One by one, Rin, Keiko, and Aaron's faces popped into view on the video call.

Sweat dripped down Rin's cheeks as the camera bounced, hints of greenery flashing behind him. Running, yet again.

In the video next to his, Keiko's black hair spread across a white pillow beneath her head. She blinked sleepily and rubbed at her face. Pulling all-nighters was typical for an assassin.

In contrast, Aaron sat at his office desk, most likely awake and working since the sun came up. His typing didn't cease despite connecting to the call.

"What's up, boss?" Rin asked, his face red.

They were all equals, yet Rin had coined the nickname "boss" for Dominic as their pseudo-leader. He had been the glue that bound them all together over the years.

"I need a favor." Dominic was going to break his promise to leave Bree alone in the best way he knew how, which meant he needed reinforcements.

Stifling a yawn, Keiko quirked an eyebrow. "Awful early for a favor."

"Not all of us live such glamorous lives as you," Aaron muttered, never once pausing his typing.

She rolled over and rested her cheek on her arm. "Oh yes, having to scrub blood and guts from one's body before downing a few Ambiens just to sleep is *so* glamorous."

At that, the accountant stopped typing and looked directly into the camera. "You take Ambien because you drink an exorbitant amount of caffeine every day. You love what you do, guts and all, and yes, attending extravagant parties to learn your marks' routines is considered glamorous."

Her lips curled into a devious smirk, revealing the slightest hint of fang. "Touché."

Rin slowed to a stop and grinned, though his chest continued to heave with deep breaths. "That's my girl."

These three could continue for hours if Dominic let them. "If you've finished with the pleasantries?"

Keiko covered her mouth with a hand, stifling another yawn. "Out with it."

Carefully avoiding any details regarding the fight due to the oath-keeper, he told them where and how he found Bree, her real name, and explained his date idea. The plan earned equal parts taunts and laughs, but they all agreed to do their part.

Now he just had to wait until evening.

The landline rang. His friends' banter fell silent as they watched him anxiously. Only one person used his landline, and it was never just to chat.

With a sigh, he lifted the receiver. He didn't keep much from his friends, so there was no need for discretion. "Yes, sir?"

"There's a large shipment coming in tonight," Ichiro said. "I need you to ensure it gets here without any trouble."

Dominic's grip on the phone tightened. "With respect, sir, can someone else go in my stead? Perhaps Kenzo? I've a prior commitment."

It was a long shot, and risky to even ask without drawing the old man's ire. But she was worth the risk.

His grandfather's voice was sharp. "What commitment?"

"A personal one."

A heavy silence fell over the line before Ichiro answered. "As much as it pains me to say, I need the best. I will not ask you again. Do not disappoint me."

Gritting his teeth, Dominic knew arguing would be futile. "As you wish."

"I'll have Akio send you the details. And, boy?"

"Yes, sir?"

"Don't fuck this up."

The line went dead.

Replacing the receiver, Dominic laughed humorlessly. He couldn't afford to fuck anything up. Unlike Kenzo and his other cousins, the old man wouldn't hesitate to kill Dominic for one wrong move.

He returned his gaze to his friends' knowing faces on the monitor. "I'll have to postpone the date."

"Call him back and tell him *no*." Keiko sat up and glared into the camera. "He treats you like shit. I mean, way more than the rest of us."

Frustration and disappointment rolled through Dominic's thoughts and emotions like thunder, but his determination to win Bree over didn't waver. He wouldn't let this setback discourage him. "This is important for the plan, but I will make this date happen sooner rather than later."

They'd spent years putting their plan into action, ensuring no one but Dominic could take over the Sato businesses. He couldn't rock the boat now with the end almost in sight. But once Ichiro officially named him as heir, he'd sink that ship faster than the Titanic.

As he wrapped up the call with his friends, he couldn't shake the feeling that winning Bree's heart had become more than just a challenge. It was as if fate had set them on a collision course, destined to change both their lives forever.

CHAPTER 13
Bree

Everyone around me was in danger. Dodging pedestrians and cars as though their lives depended on it—because they did—I didn't stop running until I reached the river. My lungs burned as much from the run as from holding back my magic, and my ragged gasps did little to ease the pain.

Fully clothed, I dove into the murky river without hesitation. The cool water embraced me, wrapping around my body like a protective shell and soothing my frayed nerves. It wasn't the salty ocean water my skin craved, but it would suffice for now.

When I was deep enough beneath the surface and sure no passing boats would see me, I released my pent-up wail. The blast of magic surged out and away from me with the force of a tsunami. The massive explosion served as a stark reminder of the burden I carried.

The fear of killing someone again would haunt me forever.

Immediately, I sucked the water's force back toward me, halting an actual tsunami from forming on the surface. With any luck, boaters and sightseers wouldn't notice anything but a minor disturbance.

My siren scream was deadly to human ears, which meant I could only release it in places like this where the sound would be muffled, or in the mountains where no one was around. It was also the reason my mother was dead.

My heart continued to race, reeling from the adrenaline and confusion that led me to this point—now and in life in general. Closing my eyes and heart against the torrent of memories and emotions, I gave myself another minute to calm down. I couldn't breathe underwater in this form, but I could hold my breath longer than any human.

As I relaxed and floated beneath the river's surface, my mind drifted back to the fight. I couldn't believe I'd just fought the Red Dragon. Fought and *won*. Sure, I'd caught him off guard with my unique type of magic, which is the real reason I won, but still. *I'd won.*

But as much as I wanted to be thrilled, I was more disappointed than anything. Maybe it was proof I'd gone mad, but I didn't want him to leave me alone. Not truly. Except dating anyone, let alone a playboy and lethal fighter like Dominic Sato, wasn't feasible in my life.

Not now, maybe never.

I'd accepted that fate when I'd made my deal with the sea witch, and for the most part, I'd never regretted it.

Until now.

I groaned and a stream of bubbles rose in front of me. I gripped the amulet around my neck tight, its edges digging into my palm painfully. The magical charm that kept me looking human also meant I could only stay under for another few moments unless I removed it.

Now wasn't the time to play mermaid. I'd released the energy without killing anyone, and now I needed to head home, back to my duties.

Swirling my hand in the water, I created a small vortex with my magic and wrapped it around me. It lifted me toward the rippling sky until I surfaced with a gasp, dragging in deep breaths of warm air. The afternoon sun bounced off the multitude of buildings surrounding the river, their reflections creating a kaleidoscope of color across the inky water.

The fight with Dominic had been wholly unexpected, but I'd gone into it determined to force him out of my life and my fantasies for good. Instead, I'd caught a glimpse of the man behind the cocky façade—one who appealed to me far more than he should have.

He was direct, sometimes to the point of arrogance, but he wasn't apologetic for going after something he wanted. His interest in me seemed genuine, though misplaced.

Add in the fact I'd used my siren abilities against another person other than Frankie for the first time in years, and it made for a potent cocktail of confusion, exhilaration, and no small amount of panic.

What a mess. I floated in the water while I tried to make sense of everything. The whirlwind of emotions continued to course through me, threatening to pull me under the surface just like the river's current.

"Hey, you okay over there?" a voice called out from a nearby dock.

Startled, I glanced over to see an older fisherman casting his line into the water.

"Uh, yeah. Just taking a swim," I called back, trying to sound casual despite my inner turmoil. Not many people swam in the Potomac thanks to the pollution. Come to think of it, swimming might be illegal. "Nice day for it."

"Suit yourself." He tipped his hat before returning to his fishing pole.

As I floated away in the gently rocking water, my thoughts wandered back to Dominic. Our bodies, locked in a fierce dance of power and desire, had blurred the lines between reality and fantasy. A part of me yearned for the excitement and connection that he offered. A big part of me.

But beneath the exhilarating surge of combat, my promise to protect Marissa lingered like an anchor. After years of hiding our true identities and struggling to keep us clothed and fed, indulging in romance wasn't a luxury I could afford.

Despite my frustration with my sister for getting me into this pickle (Frankie would be proud), I chuckled. Marissa's boundless energy and unwavering love had always been a source of strength for me, even when it led to chaos and danger, which sometimes felt like more often than not.

It was in moments like these that I realized just how much I was willing to give up for her happiness. Even if it meant sacrificing my own.

I closed my eyes and took a deep breath, relishing the silence. Relative silence in a bustling city like D.C., anyway. Here, away from prying eyes and worries, I could simply *be*.

No siren princess with expectations of marriage and offspring looming overhead.

No financial responsibilities tugging at me like a noose around my neck.

No disgusting toilets waiting to be scrubbed.

Just Bree.

"Stronger than the tide," I whispered, my words carried away by the breeze.

Each sea kingdom had a royal coat of arms and motto, but our family's was as old as time, stretching beyond our history's memory. Knowing we came from such a long lineage had always been a source of pride, and I'd done my best to be stronger than the tide every day.

I would continue to do so until I took my last breath.

With a final, longing glance at the water behind me, I swam toward shore, feeling both lighter and heavier than before. I climbed out and wrung out my clothes, knowing that no matter what the future held, I wouldn't fail my sister. And, in some strange way, that knowledge gave me the strength to face whatever challenges lay ahead.

At least now the fight was over and done. I could go back to avoiding Dominic and sticking to my routine. Keeping my distance was the smart, safe choice.

So, why did that thought leave such a bitter taste in my mouth?

BY THE TIME I MADE IT BACK TO THE GYM, MY clothes and hair were damp but no longer a sopping mess thanks to the early spring heat. I headed for the basement, glancing around the open space and hoping Dominic was still there.

It was empty.

He'd left.

Not that I blamed him. I told him to leave me alone and ran

away. He probably thought I was a coward or a weirdo. Probably both. Whatever. I didn't care what he thought.

Well, I *shouldn't* care what he thought.

"I need all the deets," Marissa's voice chirped as she jumped out of Frankie's office and into my path. She'd pulled her red hair up into a messy bun, making her blue eyes pop with her added excitement. "I can't believe you got to touch Dominic Sato instead of me."

Her cherubic, freckled face gawked at me in equal parts horror and amazement, and I almost laughed.

"That'll teach you not to miss your VIP appointments." I stepped around her. My bare, dirty feet ached as I walked, reminding me that shoes would have been nice on my impromptu jaunt through the city.

"Why do you look like a drowned squirrel?" her voice followed after me. "Did you go for a swim without me?"

I knew it was useless to try to ignore her, but exhaustion was creeping in fast. "No, I just needed a release."

"Ew, that sounds like you orgasmed."

Rolling my eyes, I descended the few steps into our underground haven. "All good there, thanks."

"Ugh, I did *not* need to know that. But also, you're a filthy liar. You haven't had sex since..." her voice trailed off. "Wait, have you ever had sex?"

Finley swam to the front of his aquarium and blinked. Seeing us both walking around here at the same time was probably unusual. My sister and I were awake at completely different times of day, or night, in her case.

I stripped off my soggy clothes and dropped them on the ground before heading to the bathroom. "Yes, Riss, I have. Not that that's any of your business."

"Aren't sisters supposed to be able to talk about this kind of stuff?"

"Not if you keep saying 'ew' and 'ugh' like a guppy." I pulled the bathroom curtain closed in her face. I didn't even have time to turn the shower on before she stomped her way in.

"That was rude, but whatever. Tell me about Dominic." Marissa folded her arms across her voluptuous chest and leaned against the pedestal sink.

I would've been envious of her curves if I wanted the kind of attention she received. But I didn't, so I was fine with the handful I had. More wasn't always better.

"He came, we talked, he left. Now, can I shower in peace?" I tested the water with my hand. Perfectly cold.

"You're wasting time delaying the inevitable, Bree. Give me the specifics."

Sliding the shower curtain closed behind me, I stepped under the cold flow of water and breathed a sigh of relief. It would never get as cold as the depths I grew up in, but if this was the best I could get for now, I'd take it.

"Fine. He asked me out on a date. I said no, and he agreed to leave me alone. End of story." There was only so much I could share with the oath-keeper binding me.

As the silence stretched on, I assumed she'd left, disappointed in one of my decisions yet again. Instead, the shower curtain flew to the side, and I stared at my sister's shocked face with equally wide eyes.

"You did *what*?"

"You heard me. I'm not explaining it again." I reached for the shampoo and started scrubbing it into my hair. The lavender scent was divine. This was one small benefit to the human world, though I'd never had to worry about my hair beneath the waves. In our true forms, salt water was more than enough.

"How can you be such an idiot?" she asked.

I blinked at her as bubbles ran down my cheeks. "Excuse me?"

"You know who he is, right? Like, not just Dominic Sato, but who the Satos are?"

Besides a family of billionaires? "Why would that even matter? I know enough to stay away."

She shook her head, her expression incredulous. "The fact that you asked that means you have no idea."

Unease crept through me, raising goosebumps. I closed my eyes and rinsed the bubbles out of my hair. "Again, why would I care? Nothing else is happening."

Her chuckle echoed through the bathroom. "Sure it's not. Do me a favor and Google him."

The bathroom curtain slid shut.

She didn't mean to use Google literally since most of the Gifted kind didn't show up in human world searches. We made sure of that. But we did have our own forums and sites online, hidden like the dark web only with magic. Using non-Gifted terms made it easier to discuss these things in public.

My curiosity got the best of me as I finished showering and turned off the water. Letting my hair air dry, I wrapped the towel around my body and padded out of the bathroom. Besides Finley, who was happily burping out bubbles in his tank, our room was empty.

Since the gym would be closed for another hour or so, as it was every weekday afternoon, I sat cross-legged on my bed and unlocked my phone. This siesta-like time provided Frankie and me with a much-needed break before the evening frenzy.

I typed Dominic's name into the search bar but paused before hitting enter. Did I really want to know what Marissa was referring to? I was never going to see him again, so who he was didn't matter.

But my curiosity was raring to go, and I wanted to know what she'd meant. *Needed* to know.

I tapped the search key.

Article after article appeared about the Sato family. My eyes widened as I read about the dragon family that ruled the supernatural underworld with an iron fist. A clawed iron fist. Multiple stories explained how Gifted authorities never had enough evidence to convict any of them.

Dominic's name and picture flashed across the screen time and again, some writers predicting he'd one day take over the Sato empire, while others were scathing in their judgment of his alleged crimes. He was the grandson of the most powerful, most brutal mob boss this city had ever seen.

He was also a murderer.

My heart thumped wildly as I clicked my phone off and clutched it to my chest.

How had I never known these things before? I glanced at the book next to me. Staying far away from the tabloids and gossip, that's how. Perhaps to my detriment. Maybe it was time to start paying attention, if only to protect myself and Marissa better.

Wow. I'd dodged a bullet. A dragon-sized bullet. Having him out of my life was definitely the right thing to do.

Ignoring an odd sense of emptiness, I slid off the bed and got dressed.

CHAPTER 14

Bree

After blowing Finley a kiss, I went upstairs to find something to eat. Frankie and Marissa were laughing about something outside the gym's office.

Grabbing a nearby mop, I stalked over and shoved the handle in my sister's face. "I'm so glad you're still here to live up to your end of the deal."

She gave the handle a look of disgust but accepted it long enough to lean it against the wall. "Fine. But I don't have long."

I caught Frankie's eye and grinned. "Long enough for me to tell you our idea."

Marissa glanced at us warily. "Why don't I like the sound of that? Or that look on your faces?"

"The gym needs money to stay afloat," I explained, slipping past them and into the office. The small fridge here was closer than my boss's apartment and held the other half of my tuna sub from earlier. I was too hungry to trek upstairs for something else. "Frankie and I came up with a fantastic idea to bring in extra funds."

The fae woman threw her hands up as she and Marissa

followed me into the office. "Oh-ho no, kiddo, this was all your idea." Her chair creaked as she sat behind her desk. "I couldn't possibly take credit."

I stuck out my tongue as I opened the fridge. "Coward."

"Out with it, Gabrielle." Marissa just about stomped her foot with each syllable.

Ha! She used my full name. I loved messing with her like this as payback. Her anger was enough to rival a dragon's.

My heart twisted at the memory of a red dragon spirit swirling around me, but I banished that thought before it gained any traction. I grabbed the wrapped-up sub and closed the fridge. "We're going to offer massages to the fighters and trainees. Right here at the club, and you, my beautiful, amazing sister, are going to be the masseuse."

Buttering her up had always worked well in my favor in the past. Hopefully, it would today, too.

Leaning back in her chair, Frankie grinned. Give her a bowl of popcorn, and she'd be ready for the show.

Marissa's jaw fell open as if her brain short-circuited. Because it probably did.

I rushed on before she could recover enough to argue. "You'll get your hours in for school, and the gym will crush its debt. Good deeds all around."

Snapping her mouth closed, she settled for glaring at me. "You are much sneakier than I give you credit for."

I took a seat and unwrapped the sub, my mouth watering as the delicious scent wafted free. Saving this half had been a great idea. "Technically, you don't give me credit for anything."

"And if I say no?" she demanded right as I took a huge bite.

Hoping for backup while I chewed, I glanced at Frankie.

My boss shrugged. "Back to the drawin' board, I guess."

Except that board was blank. I frowned at Marissa as I finished chewing and swallowed. "After everything Frankie has done for us, you would say no to helping her out?"

Scowling, she dropped into the seat beside me. "You know I hate being forced into things."

"Okay, look at it this way. Think of all the muscled, naked bodies you'll get to touch. You know some good-looking guys train here." My stomach growled, urging me to take another bite of the sub.

Thankfully, I didn't have to share this half with Finley. He'd gotten more than enough earlier.

Marissa's nose scrunched up. "Some, maybe, but it'll be just my luck to get all the wrinkly old men."

Hook, line, and sinker.

I'd won her over with that idea. Not about the old guys, but the hot ones outnumbered the old. Okay, maybe not hot-hot but dateable at the very least.

"You're our only hope," I said around a mouthful of bread and tuna.

My sister stared at me, her eyes narrowed in thought. I chewed slowly, waiting for her official decision. If she said no, I didn't know what else we could do. We were out of time and options.

"Fine," she said in a drawn-out huff. "We're not talking about massages with happy endings though, right?"

What an odd question. Massages should always end with the customer happy.

Frankie caught my perplexed expression and snorted out a laugh. "It means with a hand job, kiddo. Or a blow job for the right tip. And the answer is no. Fuck no. Most of those horndogs don't have the money for that kind of service, anyway."

"Oh."

My boss doubled over with laughter while Marissa just gave me a look of pity.

"You need to get out more." She shook her head, then pointed at me. "Also, no more mopping. This plan of yours will take up all my free time."

Cringing inside, I forced a nod. Getting out of cleaning was to be expected with Marissa, but it was a price I was glad to pay to make this plan work. She wasn't wrong about me needing to get more, but first things first.

Our future here was looking bright again. We had a plan to save our home, and nothing could stand in our way.

Famous last words.

THE NEXT MORNING, FRANKIE TASKED ME WITH cleaning the extra equipment in the storage room before we rotated everything later that night. Besides the daily sanitizing, we deep-cleaned equipment once a week. Doing so also allowed us to check for any damage or pieces that needed replacing.

However, I wasn't sure which was worse: cleaning toilets after a fight night or being stuck in a windowless room that had no air conditioning and reeked of a week's worth of stale body odor.

Three hours later, I locked the door behind me and gulped in the only somewhat better-smelling gym air. Stuck in the supply room for so long was definitely worse than the toilets.

Then I noticed the crowd.

The whole gym was abuzz with excitement. With wide eyes, I wove my way past members and toward the office. Subliminal was one of a few places in D.C. where Gifted types could mingle and chat freely, which meant I'd known most of the shifters and witches who frequented the place for years.

But today, quite a few unfamiliar faces popped up throughout the gym and talked animatedly with one another while lifting weights or punching bags. New folks weren't unheard of, but this many at once was uncommon.

Most were too involved in their conversations to notice me eavesdropping, or too used to my presence to begin with. When I finally heard enough to realize what they were discussing, my eyebrows shot toward my hairline.

Turns out, I didn't need a week to generate enough interest.

Word about our new massage offering had spread far faster and with more interest than we expected. Frankie and I had worked long into the previous evening, planning out logistics and printing posters and flyers. Thank goodness we'd doubled our initial print estimate at the last minute because it looked like every person here had a flyer in hand or tucked into a pocket already.

Marissa flirted shamelessly with some of the younger, more attractive members loitering near the front door, winking and tossing her flaming red hair over her shoulder. Today, her make-up highlighted her blue eyes, and she'd put all her assets on display with a low-cut crop top and high-waisted yoga pants.

I rolled my eyes at her antics but couldn't stop the smile tugging at my lips. At least she'd made time for this because clearly, it was working.

We'd hung a sign-up sheet on a clipboard outside the office, and as I neared the office door, my heart beat faster. A list of names covered the entire first page of open massage times.

Coconuts, this might actually work.

Not only to get the gym out of debt, but it could also help Marissa meet her school requirements faster and stay closer to where I could keep my eye on her. Plus, it might turn into a fantastic starting clientele for when she graduated. Marissa better be ready to grovel at Frankie's feet for going along with this idea.

A quick scan of the names brought an ounce of disappointment. No Dominic Sato. But really, it was for the best. Out of sight, out of mind.

Eventually.

"Who's crazy idea was this?" Calvin asked, coming up beside me and leaning on my shoulder.

Not many would lean on me that way considering I was usually dressed for scrubbing toilets and known for being a bit of a loner—compared to Marissa and Frankie, anyway—but I didn't mind the invasion of my personal space when it came to Calvin. We'd been buddies for years.

"Oh, come on, Cal. Who else is this much of a genius?" I elbowed him playfully in the ribs.

Standing just shy of six feet tall, the wizard grinned down at me. "I knew it. Only your imagination is this wild."

Although Calvin's slimmer build wasn't the typical type that frequented the gym, he was attractive in his own way. A scruffy brown beard hugged his chin, more from forgetting to shave than planned, and his dark hazel eyes almost always twinkled with merriment.

He was also one of the few wizards who'd ever joined Subliminal. Witches and wizards could be either male or female, with the main difference being how they used their magic. Whereas witches typically drew on the elements to harness their spells as needed, wizards performed complex rituals with runes and utilized wands.

Because they could store extra mana in their wands, they didn't need to rely on elemental particles being nearby like witches did. Wizards were generally considered more powerful than witches and often worked for the Gifted Interests Government, our primary governing agency.

The GIG did more than just police us, however. They also offered various services, such as lawyers, doctors, and even budding cryptozoologists like Calvin.

While he was no exception to working for the GIG, he conveniently "never heard about" the illegal fights. I was sure his superiors would catch on eventually, but for almost three years now, I'd been wrong.

"Blame my imagination on the books," I said with a shrug. "You'd be surprised how often a damsel in distress becomes her own knight in shining armor with a little creative thinking."

He chuckled. "Don't ever give up reading those fantasy books if it gives you awesome ideas like this."

Like I would ever give up reading anything. I nodded at the list. "I see you signed up."

"No way would I pass up an opportunity like this." He rubbed one of his shoulders for emphasis. "You see how brutal it is in the ring."

He didn't mean the illegal fights, of which he "knew nothing." Any gym member could reserve the ring during normal business hours to compete against another sans magic. Just fists and fury. They weren't nearly as popular as the other fights but took far less preparation and secrecy.

But little did Calvin or anyone else know, I knew exactly how brutal the ring could be from personal experience.

Frankie's fae magic allowed her to conjure up ridiculously life-like opponents for me to practice with whenever I felt the desire to punch something other than a bag. It was the only reason she knew so much about my magic.

I smiled. "I'm glad we can help you guys out this way while also helping the gym."

He slung an arm around my shoulder. "Anything for family, right?"

Knowing others felt the same way about this place warmed my heart. "You bet."

Another member called Calvin over, leaving me to contemplate the list by myself. Feeling disappointed that Dominic hadn't signed up yet was beyond absurd.

For one, he didn't train at Subliminal, not even during his fighting days. None of the dragons did.

Two, I'd told the man to leave me alone. He was obviously respecting my wishes. I should be glad of that, not frustrated.

Besides, did I want Marissa touching him instead of me?

I pursed my lips. Nope.

The good news was that it was still fairly early in the day, and many gym members kept late hours, coming in after their day jobs. I was sure the list would double if not triple by closing time. We were off to a fin-flipping-tastic start.

Frankie popped her head out of the office, saw me, then nodded toward Marissa, who was still flirting the day away by the front door. "She's gonna have those boys eatin' outta the palm of her hand in no time." A note of grudging approval marked her words. "At the rate she's goin', we'll pay off the debt within the month."

"If anyone can charm people into turning over their wallets, it's Marissa," I said wryly. "She's determined when she sets her mind to something."

If only that happened more often and with things that helped around here. You know, like cleaning.

Ah, well. Beggars couldn't be choosers.

Frankie chuckled before disappearing back into her office.

Sighing, I headed for the supply closet. My neverending list of daily chores wouldn't complete itself.

"Did you see the number of sign-ups?"

I jumped as Marissa's voice came out of nowhere. The caddy of cleaning supplies I was pulling off a shelf nearly toppled to the ground before I caught it again. "Gee-sus, Riss."

Her smirk was downright devious. "That never gets old."

I set the caddy on a lower shelf and grabbed a pair of clean gloves. Startling and scaring me were among her favorite games, ones she unfortunately played with my boss. "Yes, I saw the list. We're off to a great start."

She examined her nails while I tugged each elbow-length yellow glove on. "I think I should negotiate a higher cut."

I released a glove a little too hard, flinching when I almost punched myself in the face. "Don't you *dare*. This is to help Frankie out. To save our home. You wanna live on the street?"

She trotted after me as I grabbed the caddy and headed for the locker room. "We wouldn't have to worry about things like that if you just hooked up with Dominic."

My heart did a little skip at the idea, but I shot her a disgusted look. "One hookup isn't going to fix our money problems."

"It would if you got pregnant."

This time, I did drop the caddy. Cleaning supplies jostled together and bounced out, rolling across the ground. Down the short hallway in the main gym area, a few heads turned our way, but thankfully no one rushed to help.

"Marissa!" I hissed.

Her laugh echoed off the walls. "Don't pretend you haven't thought about it."

Yeah, okay, I might have considered dating the guy. Or rather, imagined what his magnificently naked body would feel like pressed against mine, but I most certainly had not thought of anything past that. "We're not all horny dogs like you. That's a terrible idea for so many reasons."

"The word is 'horndogs.'"

"Whatever."

"Well, if this massage idea doesn't work, I'm letting Frankie know you volunteered to make babies with Dom—"

"Shh!" I slapped my gloved hand over her mouth and glanced behind her. No one was anywhere near close enough to have heard that, but I wasn't taking any chances. "Are you out of your mind?"

With a horrified grimace, she peeled my hand off her face. "I think I'm going to be sick. You clean toilets with those."

I shook my yellow rubber finger in her face. "So don't say crazy things like that where people could overhear and get their own ideas. And don't be such a guppy. These are clean."

She scrunched her freckled nose and backed away. "It's still gross."

I bent to pick up the few escaped cleaning bottles and tucked them back into the caddy. "Don't say anything to Frankie." I stood, hoisting the caddy. "This will work."

"If you say so." Marissa's words carried after me as I entered the locker room, but she didn't follow me this time.

As usual, the stench of musty body odor slammed into me,

but I'd long since become accustomed. Since the majority of our members were shifters and therefore not especially self-conscious, we didn't bother separating men from women or any other designation.

Plus, the gym just wasn't big enough to offer more than one changing room. No one had complained yet, so we kept things as they were.

Ignoring several people in various states of undress, I got to work while thinking over my conversation with Marissa. Having babies wasn't something I'd ever seen myself doing, but I'd be lying if I said I hadn't felt a thrill of excitement when Marissa mentioned having Dominic's.

Yep. It was official.

I was certifiable.

CHAPTER 15

Bree

The next two days passed in a blur as excitement over the new massage service grew. Word had continued to spread, and even more members had come in on their off days just for a chance to sign up.

Marissa had tried to convince us to go digital with the form, allowing even more business to accumulate, but neither Frankie nor I were especially tech-savvy. We needed to be able to handle sign-ups when my sister wasn't around, which was roughly ninety-nine percent of the time.

While Frankie claimed her fae magic made all things electronic go on the fritz, I was already sixteen when we'd left home, an adult under the ocean and nearly an adult in the human world. I'd started working right away and had no time to learn new things, while Rissa had only been ten. Adapting to changes like phones and computers was easier when all your friends and schools used them.

Once, she'd even tried to convince me to read books electronically on my phone, but I'd squashed that idea with a hearty laugh and a hard nope. Nothing smelled or felt better than an actual, physical book in my hands.

Besides, I didn't want her schedule to get out of control. She still had school to finish, and if I let her have access to anything digital, she'd drop out, claiming she didn't need school when she was doing fine on her own.

Fine with our kind maybe, but she'd still need a license to practice massage therapy on humans. There weren't enough Gifted people in D.C. with the money and interest to keep her in business indefinitely.

Sighing, I turned my thoughts to the task at hand and allowed my imagination to take over. Daydreaming about my latest book boyfriend—or a certain dragon—always made the day go by faster.

I FINISHED EVERYTHING ON MY FRIDAY TO-DO LIST BY early afternoon, so I poked my head into Frankie's office, where I found her muttering at her computer screen. "Need anything before I head out to grab a late lunch?"

She peered at me over the frame of her glasses. "Someone's here to see you."

My heartbeat sped up as I glanced back at the gym. Except, I didn't see anyone looking for me. Definitely not someone I shouldn't be hoping to see.

"It's not the dragon, but I made the guy wait outside 'till you finished." She hunted for the next few keys on the keyboard and pecked at them. "Seemed too fancy to be in here."

My curiosity was officially piqued but so was my caution.

Did our father finally find us?

Pushing open the gym's front door, I squinted against the sudden brightness. Painting all the windows black and growing up beneath the waves meant I was never prepared for the sun.

Other than a man in a sleek suit and dark sunglasses standing beside a long black limo, I didn't see anyone looking for me. Whoever it was must have gotten tired of waiting.

As I moved to go back inside, the man beside the limo took a step forward and removed his sunglasses. "Ms. Johnson?"

Despite the day's warmth, goosebumps rose along my arms. I took a longer look at the man. He wasn't overly tall, but he had broad shoulders and big hands. Those bad boys could wrap around my neck easily.

I glanced up and down the street, only slightly reassured by the humans milling about. "Uh, yes?"

He reached inside his jacket pocket and withdrew a black envelope, which he handed to me.

Keeping one foot inside the gym, prepared to flee, I cracked open the envelope. The letter inside smelled like *him*. A fact I probably should not have known, but the red dragon wax seal had confirmed it anyway.

My eyes widened as I read over the invitation, then reread it two more times.

Was I still daydreaming? Were the bleach fumes making me hallucinate?

"Mr. Sato has provided his car for you this afternoon," the man in the suit said formally.

I blinked at him, then at the limo. His *car*, huh? "That's very generous, but Mr. Sato agreed to leave me alone after we... after his last visit."

An uncomfortable prickling sensation rolled over my skin, and I rubbed my arm. The oath-keeper must have been letting me know I was too close to discussing the fight. Not that I wanted to discuss it with a stranger, but it would be Dominic's fault if I accidentally did.

The suit nodded. "He asked me to apologize for not following through with your agreement, but he will explain in person."

I snorted. "If he was so set on breaking his word, why didn't he come in person?"

"He presumed you'd want to change for your date first."

I glanced down at my faded black leggings and a no-longer-white tank top with permanent pit stains. Not exactly date material. "Yeah, no, I'm not dressed for a date because I don't date."

Crinkles formed around the man's kind eyes. "He presumed that as well, which is why we'll start with a trip to a salon."

I was pretty sure this was the bleach fumes talking. "I'm sorry, what?"

"He's rented the entire salon out for your private use and has provided a selection of the latest fashions to choose from."

Nope. Not happening. "I'm afraid you'll have to disappoint Mr. Sato. I'm not interested. If you'll excuse me, some of us have real work to—"

A hand pushed me roughly out the door, and I stumbled forward. I spun around to find Frankie's grinning face in the doorway.

"Oops. Bye!" She cackled once before her face disappeared inside, pulling the door shut quickly.

When I tried the handle, it didn't budge. I banged on the metal frame of the door. "Frankie! Come on, open up!"

"What was that? Can't hear you," her only somewhat muffled voice drifted through the glass windows.

Grumbling, I turned back to face the suit.

He smiled gently and opened the limo's back door. "Air conditioning and fresh water are waiting for you, Ms. Johnson. My name is Samson should you need anything else."

Since I always kept the basement door locked and didn't carry keys while inside the gym (because why would I?), I had a choice to make. I could stand out here until Frankie caved and let me in, barge my way in if someone opened the door to leave, or go get dolled up to meet Dominic Sato.

Since Frankie was even more stubborn than I was and, for some unknown reason, supporting this kidnapping, I had a strong suspicion she wouldn't let anyone inside leave anytime soon. That or she'd find a way to magic them out. The sun was already hot on my pale skin, which only left option C.

Pride was a hard thing to swallow sometimes, but going along with this plan would allow me the opportunity to give Dominic a real piece of my mind. He would regret kidnapping me, no matter how many fancy things he threw my way.

I didn't need or want his charity.

"Please call me Bree." I smiled politely at Samson and slipped into the limo.

As promised, cool air kissed my skin as soon as I slid across the seat. A bottle of cold water waited for me, as did a chilled bottle of champagne, already uncorked with a full glass beside it. The extraordinary wealth and privilege on display practically assaulted my senses.

There could be worse ways to spend my afternoon before chewing someone out.

I helped myself to the bubbly and sank back into the luxurious, black leather seat. I'd never sat on anything this comfortable in the human world, and I couldn't help but wonder how much something like this cost to maintain.

Absurd amounts of money wasted on a mode of transportation that was slowly killing our planet. I scrunched up my nose and set the champagne flute back.

Ridding the world of one extra-long car wouldn't do much in the grand scheme of things, but landlubbers loved having every new trinket and gadget that came on the market. So many materialistic things, when there were other options like public transportation and recycled products.

My gaze drifted out the window, where the busy sidewalks flew by. Used food wrappers and empty cans and bottles littered the roads and blocked sewage drains, strengthening my point.

Leaving our home had been my idea, but I wish I'd known more about this world before I came. Not that there were many other options to escape our father, but at least I'd have come in knowing rather than realizing it after the fact.

I wasn't sure how that made a difference, but somehow it did.

When the limo finally slowed to a stop along a curb, I peered up at the storefront. We were parked in front of the city's most exclusive spa and salon, La Belle Vie. Yes, even I'd heard of the place. Of course he would pick this place.

I gritted my teeth, steeling myself for an afternoon of lavish extravagance that was sure to end in frustration—*Dominic's* frustration. The thought made me smile, and I relaxed a bit.

Samson opened the car door and offered his hand to help me out. I eyed it for a moment before accepting, reminding myself that he wasn't responsible for this foolish venture.

"Shall we go in, Ms. Johnson?" His genuine smile reached his eyes, melting some of my resolve. "Your treatments await."

Treatments. As in more than one. This was going to be a long afternoon.

Inside, I was ushered into an elegant waiting room. Soft, muted colors adorned the walls, creating an atmosphere of understated elegance. A crystal chandelier hung like a work of art in the center of the room, casting an inviting glow that bathed the space in a soft, golden light.

A woman in a crisp white blouse and pinned-up jet-black hair approached, her smile professionally pleasant. "Ms. Johnson, we are so pleased to have you with us today. Mr. Sato has arranged a wonderful treatment plan, followed by styling, and your choice of attire from our designer collection for your date this evening."

"There seems to have been a mistake, ma'am," I said with a tight smile. "I'm not interested in any of this."

"Please, call me Amy, and accept my sincerest apologies for any confusion." Her smile never wavered. "However, if you'll allow me to point out, everything has already been paid for and arranged. Perhaps it would be best to enjoy yourself for now, and you can express your concerns to Mr. Sato in person after?"

In other words, I was stuck. Tides, he was good.

I sighed, resigned to my fate. "Fine. Do your worst."

"Excellent." She beamed. "This way, please."

The sleek glass doors Amy led me to slid open with a gentle whoosh, revealing the interior. My resentment faded into wide-eyed amazement as I took in the lavish space.

A rectangular pool stretched across the heart of the room, its surface adorned with floating rose petals. Soft ripples danced across the water's surface, reflecting the serene atmosphere.

Surrounding the pool, plush white lounges beckoned guests to relax and unwind, and soft-looking towels and robes embellished each lounge. My hands itched to sink into their fluffy embrace.

The walls were adorned with tasteful artwork, and ambient music played in the background, adding to the sense of tranquility.

At one end of the vast room, a sleek bar boasted a range of artisanal teas and freshly squeezed juices. An attendant stood beside an espresso machine, ready to craft custom beverages. Today, that meant just for me.

Amy guided me to an open door leading into a private treatment room and smiled. "Your day starts here."

When in Rome, as they say.

At least, I was pretty sure it was Rome.

After I stripped and settled onto a padded table, two attendants got to work, kneading scented oils into my skin and soothing my aching muscles. Tension bled from my body as I gave myself over to their practiced hands.

Marissa was a talented masseuse but nowhere near this good. Based on her instructors' gushing praise, I had a sneaking suspicion she cut corners when she practiced on me. What a brat.

By the time I emerged from the spa—scrubbed, buffed, and polished to perfection—my annoyance with Dominic had almost vanished. I felt relaxed and decadent, ready to face whatever the evening held. Even spending time with an arrogant dragon couldn't dampen my good mood now.

I could take on the world.

Wearing one of the fluffy white robes that felt as good as I'd hoped, I followed an attendant to another large room. As promised, the stylist waiting for me there presented a selection of designer outfits in expensive fabrics and a range of styles. Despite myself, I was impressed with Dominic's taste.

I browsed as if knowing what was in fashion and eventually selected a deep blue dress that clung to my slight curves before flaring at the knees. I paired it with kitten heels that didn't make me wobble too much.

The woman expertly styled my hair in loose curls and brushed on some makeup before handing me a small clutch to finish the look. Inside was a mirror and the lipstick she'd used on me.

What a lovely touch.

I hardly recognized myself in the mirrors surrounding me. When had I last dressed up like this, like the carefree socialite I once was?

Back home, we donned attire made of seaweed, clamshells, and sometimes even gems and trinkets from shipwrecks. Every activity had its dress code or preferred style.

Admiring my reflection, I looked confident and ready for war.

Dominic wouldn't know what hit him.

"I hope you have an evening as lovely as you look, Ms. Johnson." Amy assessed my choices with a smile—I'd passed. "Samson is waiting outside to take you to the restaurant."

Her use of the driver's name spoke of a familiarity between them, and I wondered how often Dominic brought women here before dates. My resentment returned tenfold.

Lovely wasn't the word I'd choose for what was about to come. I strode out to the limousine on unfamiliar heels, smoothing the dress over my hips and praying I wouldn't fall flat on my face.

Samson opened the limousine door, and I slid inside.

"Let's get this over with." The bite had returned to my words, but my frustration wasn't directed at the driver.

I'd almost fallen for Dominic's charms, and I hadn't even seen him yet. He was going to regret breaking his word.

If only I hadn't been such a dope.

CHAPTER 16

Bree

By the time Samson stopped the limo outside an unfamiliar, upscale restaurant near the White House, my boiling anger had reduced to a simmer. I still planned to give the dragon a piece of my mind, but at least I wouldn't sound like a crazy woman while doing it.

That was the goal, anyway. Fingers crossed I could pull it off.

Besides, I couldn't turn down a free meal and some decent wine for once. Who knew when I'd have the opportunity again? They better be willing to box up any leftovers, too. I didn't care how tacky that was for a place like this.

The door opened, and the driver offered his hand.

I stepped out of the limo. "Thank you, Samson. I hope he pays you well."

His brown eyes twinkled with amusement as I tucked the borrowed clutch beneath my arm. "That he does, Ms. Johnson. Enjoy your evening."

I took a deep breath and entered the restaurant.

A sparkling chandelier illuminated the foyer in a warm glow. Dark wood flooring stretched from the door to the lavish dining room behind the host's podium. The murmur of conversation mostly drowned out the music playing from the speakers, and pink and white floral arrangements added a lovely scent.

A hallway opened to the right, which I assumed led to the bathrooms, and an elevator waited to the left.

The woman standing behind the podium looked up and smiled. "Good evening. Do you have a reservation?"

Talk about a stroke of luck. She had no idea who I was. Now was my chance to get away.

As I turned to escape, I bumped into a man's massive chest. Mortified at my clumsiness, I took a step back. "Oh! Excuse me."

"She's dining with Mr. Sato," the man said to the host, though his grin was directed at me.

Surprisingly, I recognized his dark tousled hair and ridiculously sculpted physique. It was the man I'd met at Dominic's penthouse for the massage, thinking it was Dominic himself. I narrowed my eyes. "I see he just loves to get his cronies to do all his dirty work."

The man's dark eyes widened, and then he laughed so hard tears nearly spilled down his cheeks. "Oh, yeah, I get Nic's interest now. Cronies. Ha!"

My cheeks flushed with heat. "If you'll excuse me..."

As I tried to step around him toward the exit, the man blocked my way. "Trust me, nothing beats the view up there. You have to check it out before you go."

Apparently, my fancy kidnapping hadn't ended yet. I could probably scream and get away, but yelling at Dominic in a sophisticated, non-crazy way was still high on my priority list. Plus, my curiosity was getting the best of me. "Up where?"

The host appeared at my side and held out her hand toward the open elevator. "If you'll follow me?"

Sighing for what was probably the hundredth time that day, I cast a final glare at the man blocking the door. He simply winked as I entered the elevator.

Eight floors up, the elevator doors slid open, and I stepped onto the restaurant's rooftop deck. A lattice pergola covered part of the terrace's tables and chairs, but the rest remained open to the clear night sky.

String lights draped around the perimeter, defining the seating area, and candles on each table provided just enough additional light to enjoy the meal and company without ruining the view. The White House stood across the street, its stately elegance only partially muted at night.

Near the elevator, a restaurant employee stood behind a bar, drying wine glasses. He smiled but didn't make a move to show me where to go. He didn't have to. There was only one other person on this rooftop terrace, and he was the real view.

Standing with his back facing me, Dominic had one hand tucked casually into the pocket of his black slacks as he gazed out into the night. He wore a red button-down shirt, though he'd rolled the sleeves up to his elbows.

"Enjoy your evening," the host said, and the elevator door closed behind me with a ding.

When the Red Dragon turned to face me, all the angry words I'd planned to say disappeared. In the soft lighting, he took my breath away. His magnetic presence enveloped me, called me to him like the sweetest songs of the ocean.

His whiskey-colored eyes locked onto mine, and the world around us faded away. "You clean up nicely, princess. I almost didn't recognize you without your mop."

Whatever spell his gaze held over me popped like a bubble. He might know what I was after witnessing my magic in action, but that didn't mean he knew *who* I was. If he did, then the oath-keeper better do its job and keep those very kissable lips sealed tight.

I scowled. "Don't call me that."

He feigned an apologetic look but amusement danced within his gorgeous eyes. "Of course. What would you like me to call you?"

"A cab to go home, please."

His eyebrows shot up before he laughed. "So polite even when you're angry." He strode toward me, a confident swagger in each step, and swept his gaze over me.

My skin was on fire everywhere his gaze fell. Which was literally my entire body. "So annoying even when you're trying to be charming. What happened to following through with our deal? Why am I here?"

"I agreed to stop harassing you." The distance between us closed rapidly. "You never said not to take you on a date."

Was he being obtuse on purpose? "That's semantics."

As he drew near, the warm scent of a campfire drifted closer, of mouthwatering cedar embers and spiced hot cocoa. I could just drown in that scent.

My heart hammered in my chest. My instincts demanded I step back, away from the dangerous dragon, but I refused to give him the satisfaction of seeing how he affected me.

Or maybe I just wanted him that close.

"Got better plans for the evening?" He tilted his head to the side. "A new book perhaps?"

I blushed. Frankie and her big fae mouth. "A man who doesn't read isn't a man worth knowing."

He grinned. "I believe you'll find my library and fondness for reading to be an attractive quality."

I perked up at the idea of a library, but I still had questions that needed answers. "What I don't find attractive is you avoiding my questions. Why am I here, Dominic?"

A warm breeze ruffled my dress and teased the strands of my hair into a dance. My pulse sped up as his gaze tracked the movements like a predator does with his prey. I knew that if I tried to run, he would chase me and enjoy it.

Maybe I would, too.

"You're here because I would like to get to know you better, Gabrielle."

"It's just Bree. What if I don't want to get to know *you*?" I shot back.

"Something tells me you want to be here as much as I want you here, Just Bree." Finally taking a few steps backward, he stopped beside the only set table and pulled a chair out. "Let's find out while we eat. You must be starving."

As if on cue, my stomach growled. I clutched my handbag tighter beneath my arm as if it would curb my hunger. "Does this whole kidnapping thing usually work for you?"

"To be honest, I've never had to resort to such tactics." Smiling in a seductive way that unsettled as much as excited me, he moved another few steps back until he stood by the other chair. As if giving me distance would make me feel safe enough to sit. "One evening, that's all I ask of you, Bree. Indulge me. Please?"

Ugh. He just had to go and say "please" like that, all sweet and innocent, and my traitorous body just had to melt as a result. But if anyone asked, I'd blame it on the opportunity for a delicious free meal. I mean, it better be free.

I held my chin up and slid onto the chair he'd pulled out. "Fine. But you better not try to split the bill. I can't afford a single drink at a place like this."

He scoffed as he sat across from me. "When I invite someone to dine with me, it's always my treat."

"Speaking of which, how often do you treat kidnapped women to spa days before dinner?" I asked.

He gave me a funny look. "Another first."

"The kidnapping or the spa?"

"Both."

I rolled my eyes. "Sure it was. Samson and Amy were on a first-name basis."

His grin made my stomach flip-flop. "I may not treat women to the spa, but I certainly treat myself regularly. I've been a valued member at La Belle Vie for the past five years, and Samson has always accompanied me."

Well, that made sense. Any remaining anger I held onto fizzled out. "Oh."

"Massages are a necessity when training and fighting."

"I wouldn't know," I said with a slight shrug.

His gaze continued to track my every movement. "Surely you benefit from your sister's training?"

I let out a laugh and lifted my wine glass, glad to see it was already full and waiting for me. "I realized today she's been cutting corners with me."

"Is she your only sister?" He lifted his glass and tilted it slightly in my direction. "To second chances."

"Is it a second chance if I've been kidnapped?" Despite my teasing words, I mirrored his gesture before taking a sip.

Oh my. Decent wine was entirely too modest of a description. This was heaven. The literal nectar of the gods. Maybe I could get a bottle to go. I wasn't above stealing one either.

"Yes, my only sister. I'm not sure I could handle more than one like Marissa."

His grin was contagious. "I don't blame you."

Although, Frankie was a bit like a sister. Which reminded me... "How did you get Frankie on board?"

"What did that fae woman do?"

"She locked me out of the gym when your driver arrived."

His surprised laugh sent the butterflies in my stomach into a flurry. "I wish I could take credit for that ingenious move, but that was classic Frankie. As unpredictable as D.C. weather."

Oh, she was definitely going to be in trouble now. I wasn't so sure she thought I would win in a fight against the Red Dragon when she'd suggested it. Maybe she'd hoped I would lose and have to go on this date in the first place. Although, why she would care enough to lock me out was beyond me.

"What about you?" I asked, hoping to keep the conversation off my personal life as much as possible. "Any siblings?"

He shook his head. "Only child."

"Ah, no wonder you're spoiled rotten," I said playfully.

A brief moment of pain or sadness crossed his face before he flashed his disarming grin again. "Guilty as charged."

The momentary vulnerability was intriguing. I eyed him, trying to figure out why my comment had affected him that way. "Are your parents proud of all that you've accomplished in life?"

He swirled the wine in his glass and shrugged. "I wouldn't know. They both died when I was young. My mother during childbirth."

Crap on a sea biscuit. I'd completely forgotten reading

about that during my internet stalking. Was it stalking, though, if it was public knowledge?

My heart ached for him. Without thinking, I reached across the table and placed my hand on his. "I'm so sorry if I've stirred up sad memories. I know what it's like to lose a parent."

As I started to slide my hand back, he captured my palm in his. He stroked the back of my hand with his thumb, sending wildfire racing through my body.

"It is what it is," he said softly. "Tell me what happened to yours."

Gulping down the immediate flood of shame and grief, I wrenched my hand free. I tried to cover up my discomfort by pretending to scratch my arm. "Just a wrong place, wrong time type of thing. But we were talking about you and your accomplishments. How'd you get into fighting?"

His gaze studied my face. "You're very good at that."

I raised an eyebrow. "Good at what?"

"Deflecting."

My pulse sped up, and I smiled nervously, hoping it looked normal. Talking about my life meant lying outright or by omission, neither of which I wanted to do tonight. "I'm just polite, but should we get the elephant out of the room?"

"The elephant?"

I glanced over my shoulder to make sure the server was still behind the bar. "You know, what you saw during the fight."

"What did I see?"

"You know, my magic."

He tilted his head to the side, studying me. "Do you wish to discuss it?"

Well, that was hardly what I expected him to say. While I didn't think he'd be star-struck, I did assume he'd be interested in hearing more about what I was. Sirens on land were a rarity. The fact that he was leaving the decision up to me felt... good.

"No."

"Then we won't."

So matter-of-fact and so incredibly sexy. "I'm more interested in hearing more about the life of the infamous Red Dragon." I waggled my eyebrows. "I watched you fight for years, you know."

"I knew you were a bit of a stalker." He grinned at my fierce blush. Obviously, he wasn't wrong. "Try not to judge me too harshly from my fighting days. I had to win over crowds with a mostly fictitious persona."

"So you're saying you're not an arrogant playboy?"

His smile practically melted me on the spot. "Not to those who matter the most."

My heart thumped against my ribs. Like during the massage I'd given him, he was opening up to me, revealing a side I'd never expected from someone like him. I didn't want to like the idea that I might be special to him somehow, but I did. I liked it a lot.

Of course, this could all be part of his lure to get women into bed with him. But then again, I doubted he'd ever have to go to such lengths for a one-night stand. Not that I was opposed to such an idea either. A night with the Red Dragon was sure to be...memorable.

The elevator door dinged and opened, saving me from entertaining any more of *those* thoughts. A server in a white polo and crisp black pencil skirt stepped out and approached our table, carrying two plates. She smiled. "Good evening, Mr. Sato, Ms. Johnson."

Wow. I hadn't expected them to know my name. I was a nobody.

She set the plates in front of us. "For your first course this evening, we have sous vide octopus salad with heirloom tomatoes and basil vinaigrette. Please let Scott," she gestured to the server behind the bar, "know if you need anything before the next course."

With that, she backed away and returned to the elevator.

My mouth watered as I stared at the food in front of me. No, not just food. This was actual art. A masterpiece. I almost didn't want to destroy it by eating it. Almost, but my stomach won out, forcing me to pick up my knife and fork.

"Have you tried octopus before?" Dominic asked, following my lead.

"Yes, but my usual meals involve a microwave or come from a can." I wasn't ashamed of how we lived. We'd chosen to leave a life of luxury behind, and I worked hard to provide the little we had. He didn't need to know I'd eaten more octopuses in my childhood than he'd have in his entire life.

"Sounds like my childhood." He smiled. "Chef Boyardee was the only chef I knew back then. My dad wasn't exactly talented in the kitchen."

Chuckling, I took a bite of the salad. Immediately, my senses were overwhelmed. The chef had achieved a perfect tenderness with the octopus, and a hint of smoky flavor mixed with the vibrant tomatoes.

Even while chewing, my mouth watered.

I let out a small groan. "This is the most amazing thing I've ever put in my mouth."

Dominic's eyes narrowed into a hungry look, and a smirk tugged at the corners of his lips. "Is that right?"

As I realized the innuendo I'd unintentionally spoken, a flush crept up my neck. "Does your mind always go straight to the gutter?"

A teasing glimmer danced in his gaze. "Life's more interesting that way. So tell me, what made you want to take up fighting?"

I took another bite and chewed, giving myself time to contemplate a response without giving too much away. "I suppose you could say it's my way of finding strength, of proving to myself that I can overcome any challenge, you know?"

He nodded. "I understand that. I've always been drawn to the thrill of a challenge. It's about pushing beyond your limits, finding your true potential."

As we continued to learn more about each other throughout dinner, I found myself relaxing and opening up more than I ever had, other than with Frankie or Marissa. He was so easy to talk to and simply grinned at or laughed away my awkward moments, which were plenty.

Not once did he make me feel less than for my love of reading and needing time alone. I was starting to believe him when he said he'd never met anyone like me before, and for some odd reason, he liked that about me.

I liked that about him, too.

The main course was another octopus dish, this time grilled and paired with saffron risotto and roasted garlic aioli. I had never eaten such decadent foods in my life, not even at the palace. We simply couldn't prepare foods the same way—with fire.

After the last course was cleared, Dominic scooted his chair next to mine so we were both gazing out over the city. We fell into a comfortable silence, sipping wine and taking in the beautiful night air.

I closed my eyes and smiled as the breeze curled around me, bringing with it the slightest hint of rain. When I opened my eyes again, Dominic was staring at me. I couldn't decipher his expression, but my heart skipped a beat. "What?"

"You seem to find joy in the littlest things."

I raised an eyebrow. "Is that bad?"

He shook his head but his gaze dipped to my lips. "The opposite. It's incredibly attractive. Everything about you is."

Realizing we were close enough to kiss, my breath hitched in my throat.

This was it.

CHAPTER 17

Dominic

Dominic clenched his jaw, finding it exceedingly difficult to resist tasting what was sure to be the most delectable dessert of his entire life. Bree's desire for him to kiss her drifted from her body in mouthwatering waves.

Making her fantasy a reality would happen soon. He wanted to taste every inch of her body.

But this wasn't the place, and this wasn't the moment.

Not yet.

A stroke of luck arrived in the form of the bartender, even if Dominic wanted to strangle him for the interruption.

Scott reached across the table to fill their wine glasses.

Before she could mask her disappointment, Bree dropped her gaze and frowned. It was a look Dominic never wanted to see on that gorgeous face again. He would make sure her disappointment didn't last long.

The server poured the last of the wine. "Would you like another bottle?"

"No, thank you." Dominic pushed back his chair and

stood. "Let José know the service and food were as impeccable as ever."

The server beamed at the praise and retreated behind the bar.

Dominic offered his hand to Bree.

Raising an eyebrow, she took his hand and let him guide her to her feet. He pulled her closer, taking advantage of the moment to feel more of her body touching his. Like during the massage, her cool touch soothed his dragon's inner fire.

But it also fanned the flames of desire.

She looked up at him, her gaze as deep and soulful as the ocean. This close, her scent wrapped around him, salty and sweet, holding him captive.

Gods above, he wanted her, wanted that gaze locked on his as he thrust into her, fulfilling her needs night after night. He would be patient, knowing the wait would be worth it. But knowing didn't make it any easier.

"Well, thanks for dinner," she said, though she made no effort to move away from him.

He grinned, enjoying the way her skin always flushed when he did. "The night's not over yet, darlin'. I still need to know more about you."

She bit her lip in a way that made his entire body stiffen with sudden need, but then took a step back. "Despite the kidnapping and forced pampering, tonight was lovely. Thank you. I'll make sure everything I've borrowed gets returned."

"They're yours to keep, a gift."

"I couldn't possibly accept that kind of gift. You've seen where I live, the work I do." She gestured to her dress and clutch. "They deserve a happier home, with someone who can enjoy them."

"We'll just have to find another place for you to wear them." Although he'd much prefer them on his floor and Bree naked on his bed.

"Um, no, I think not. I'm sure you have a flock of women lining up on your doorstep, ready and willing to date you." Her smile was sad. "You know, those who are more suited to your lavish lifestyle."

"That's where you're wrong."

"Is that so?"

"Indeed. I don't date."

"Well, that's kind of confusing." Her eyebrows drew together. "Then why'd you call this a date?"

"Because you are the exception," he said, watching for her reaction. And when it came, it was as glorious as he'd hoped for.

Her eyes widened and her pink lips parted ever so slightly with an inhaled breath. A flush rose along her collarbone and neck, rising to her cheeks. She was absolute perfection."I'm not sure I understand. Why in the world would you want to date *me*?"

He cocked his head to the side. "Do you think so poorly of yourself?"

"No, but I'm also not an idiot. You could date any woman you set your sights on." She narrowed her eyes, and he could *feel* her indignation rising like a surging wave. Her sister wasn't the only one with a temper.

Marissa's anger was sure to be as quick to withdraw as it was to rise, but Dominic somehow knew that Bree's would be different. It would develop slowly and build over time, until the power of her wrath crashed into her target with the force of a hurricane. The damage left in her wake would be catastrophic.

Yet, despite the destruction, he would stand in awe of her strength and beauty.

"Is this some sort of game for you? A bet to see if you can make the poor girl fall for you? Slumming it for a night?"

Her words struck him like a punch to the stomach. "You are unlike any woman I've ever met, Bree. You intrigue me, challenge me. Hell, you *avoid* me." He swept his gaze over her face as the wave within her withdrew and softened her features. "I find myself thinking of you more often than not, wondering what it is you're doing and what makes you happy. I want to know everything about you, something I've never wanted from a woman before."

Her gaze dropped to the ground, but he tipped her chin back up, needing her to see the truth in his face. Drowning in the depths of those ocean-hued eyes for the rest of his life would be heaven enough, since he was surely damned to Hell.

"Something tells me there's so much more to you than meets the eye," he added quietly.

"That could be true for most people." She smiled, but there was a guarded edge to her expression. That edge had shown up several times that night.

Most people were quite transparent, which made her secrets even more tempting to unravel. He would peel back the layers and discover what had caused that guarded expression, then grind that reason into nothing but pulp.

"Maybe, but I'm willing to slum it with you for a while longer, darlin', if you'll do me the honor." He winked and held out his arm.

As she took his arm, she pursed her lips but failed at hiding her amusement. "Fine, but tell me, does calling a woman 'darlin'' actually work for you?"

Dominic led her to the elevator. "You know, I've never asked. Does it work for you?"

"I haven't decided yet," she said as the door slid shut.

THE NEXT PART OF DOMINIC'S PLAN FOR THE EVENING included a stroll down the National Mall toward the Jefferson Memorial. The memorial was one of his favorite places in the city, especially during spring when the cherry blossoms surrounding the Tidal Basin bloomed.

His friends would ensure there were no interruptions, which, being related to Ichiro Sato, happened more frequently than he'd like.

As they walked the few blocks to the National Mall, Dominic pointed out little-known features of the city. He'd studied D.C. for years, fascinated by its history and politics, past as well as current. It was one of the few interests he'd pursued for himself while growing up.

When he mentioned that at least 168 different languages were spoken by city residents, Bree's eyes widened, sparkling with genuine interest. Once again, she was proving far different from any woman he'd considered dating in the past, most of whom feigned interest or changed the subject to more mundane topics.

In the center of the Mall, the Washington Monument towered before them. Well-placed uplighting cast majestic shadows across the structure that honored the founding and first president of this country.

Beside him, Bree gasped and pointed into the darkened fields surrounding the monument. "What are those?"

He looked where she pointed but saw little more than grass and fireflies. "What?"

"The little lights dancing around."

"You mean the fireflies?"

She took a hesitant step toward one, holding a hand out as if encouraging it to land. The little bug disappeared, and she let out a surprised laugh. "I've never seen them in person before."

Dominic stood mesmerized, watching her laugh and twirl among the twinkling, dancing lights. She was beautiful and so innocent of this world. Some might see her behavior as naïveté or immaturity, but he knew it was because of where she grew up —deep beneath the waves.

An intense desire to protect her from anything that might take that purity away rose unbidden. He would kill anyone who tried.

And yet, a shadow of doubt crept into his thoughts. Not about her, she was perfection itself. She was unlike anyone else in his life, someone he wanted to treasure above all others. But he was a Sato.

A killer and a monster.

For all his sins, did he even deserve her?

Cupping his hands, he caught one of the fireflies easily. "Look."

She stepped closer until he could feel her cool breath on his arm. Slowly, he opened his hands to reveal the tiny bug resting on his palm, and her eyes widened in a look of awe.

"What a magical little thing." She smiled ruefully as it lifted into the air and flew away, her gaze following its trail. "We had similar creatures back home..."

They were so close, the tiny flecks of silver ringing her otherwise deep blue irises sparkled like diamonds as she looked up at him. Everything around him faded away until there was only her.

Just Bree.

Dominic slipped his hand behind her neck and drew her to him, claiming her lips with his. He'd waited long enough, and the moment couldn't be more right. As their lips touched, ecstasy like he'd never known filled his entire being, drawing a groan from deep within.

She tasted as sweet and salty as her unique scent, of ocean breezes on a hot summer's day. A perfect, tantalizing mixture of his favorite childhood memories and everything good in this world.

She tasted like home.

Her lips parted beneath his, inviting him to explore further.

Their tongues danced together in a way that was as familiar as the city around them. He wrapped his arms around her tiny waist, holding her tightly to him and never wanting to let her go.

Moaning into his mouth, she slid her arms around his neck and pressed her supple body into his.

A growl escaped his lips, and he sucked in her bottom lip before pulling his head back. He stared into her dazed eyes, lost in everything she was. "Have I gone mad or are you real?"

She answered him by drawing his mouth back to hers and kissing him deeply.

When he finally surfaced again, he ran his nose down her neck, breathing in her delicious scent. He nibbled gently on the soft skin at the base of her throat. "Come home with me tonight. I want to devour every last inch of you."

Gripping his arms, she let out the smallest whimper of pleasure that strained the front of his pants.

Before she could answer, his phone buzzed in his pocket.

Only one person would be calling tonight, and ignoring that man wasn't an option.

Fuck.

Dominic sighed and stepped back, putting physical distance between them if he had any hope of letting her go that night. He ran a hand through his hair, frustration and anger clutching him tight.

Although her eyes were bright with desire, her eyebrows drew together in a look of confusion.

He pulled out his buzzing phone. "I have to take this. One moment."

Disappointment swept across her expression before she smothered it and nodded. "Of course."

Twice in one night, he'd disappointed her, a fact that had his dragon writhing and ready to kill.

The call was quick but the job would not be. Ichiro demanded his services at the last minute, which meant something had gone wrong. Jou growled and writhed in agitation as Dominic slipped his phone back into his pocket. This was not how he envisioned their night ending.

Bree studied his face. "Is everything okay, Dominic?"

"No, but only because I have to go deal with someone else's mistake."

"I understand."

Grabbing her waist, he yanked her closer and cupped her face. He drank in her sharp intake of breath and ran his thumb across her beautifully swollen lips. "Understand that I will make them pay for this interruption. Next time, I plan on claiming what's mine—fully."

He lowered his face to hers and kissed her softly but deeply. When he let her go at last, he took a moment to memorize the delicate angles of her face. "And from now on, I'd prefer you call me 'Nic.' I'll have Samson bring the car around."

Her lips twisted into a cute smirk. "You have an interesting definition of the word 'car,' *Nic*."

As his dragon simmered and hissed within, demanding he forsake his grandfather and the family business and take Bree back to his bed, Dominic knew that this woman would change his world.

Only, he didn't know if her presence would destroy everything he'd worked so hard to achieve. Years of careful planning and strategic alliances.

But did he care?

Not one bit.

CHAPTER 18

Bree

As the limousine drove away from the gym, I felt like I was walking on water. The night hadn't been anything like I'd expected. It had been truly and utterly magical.

A fairytale come to life.

Except the prince in my story turned out to be a dangerous criminal from a ruthless dragon family. I wasn't sure how I felt about that yet, but I didn't want logic to ruin my night.

My brain could overanalyze it tomorrow. Tonight, I would listen to my heart.

Smiling, I pressed my fingers to my lips. The memory of Dominic's kisses lingered, a tantalizing reminder of our evening and what could have been that sent electric pulses straight to my core.

If only he hadn't gotten that phone call.

I opened the gym door, grateful to find it unlocked at last. As much as I wanted to berate Frankie for locking me out of the gym earlier and forcing me on that date, she'd obviously done the right thing. Her reasons didn't even matter anymore.

Before I stepped inside, a chill spider-walked up my spine.

Someone was watching me, I was sure of it. And they were close. I spun around, prepared to fight.

The sidewalk and street were empty.

My pulse pounded in my ears as I searched the shadows for any sign of movement. But other than the streetlights, nothing changed. This late, I was alone.

I waited another minute, assuming I was wrong about the sensation, but also hoping someone would show themselves and prove I wasn't paranoid for no reason. Unfortunately, it seemed like I was wrong. Paranoia had struck again.

With a final glance up and down the street, I went inside and locked the door behind me. Frankie's office was the only light on.

Grinning as a rare opportunity presented itself, I slipped off my heels to avoid clacking across the concrete floor. I wanted to scare her as payback. Not only for earlier that day but for all the times she'd gotten the jump on me.

I cradled my sandals in one hand and tiptoed closer. My footsteps were silent as I crossed the empty space and passed the boxing ring, closing in on her office.

Suddenly, Frankie's voice rang out, and I just about jumped out of my skin.

"You know I don't have that kind of money just layin' around," she hissed.

The fae woman's usual sarcastic tone was angry and urgent. Whoever she was talking to, the conversation was not going well.

I stopped outside the door, just out of sight. My stomach churned as guilt wormed its way through.

Eavesdropping on something like this wasn't something I would normally do, but I also didn't want to interrupt what seemed to be an important discussion. The only way to my room meant crossing her line of sight, and I wasn't sure how she'd react if she saw me.

"You can't just change dates like that," she said, exhaustion evident in her tone. "That's not the way deals work."

I heard a scratching sound inside, but I couldn't tell what was making it.

"Mmhmm, and I'm just supposed to be okay with that? C'mon, man. This is my home."

She snorted and the sound of her phone slamming shut nearly startled me enough to gasp. Thanks to her lack of tech-savviness, she was one of the few left in the world with an actual flip phone—the original kind.

Her chair creaked. "Fuck me sideways, backwards, and everywhere in between."

Well, that was a new one.

I peeked around the corner to find Frankie's head in her hands, her elbows on the desk. A hunting knife lay beside her right elbow, and a brand new "X" had been carved into the wood. It was one of many such designs, a visible outlet for her anger.

"Boo?"

A blade thunked into the doorframe next to my head. I yelped and threw myself sideways, banging into the wall.

"You're lucky I realized it was you at the last second." Frankie's narrowed violet eyes relaxed, and her irises faded back to brown. "Get my knife, will ya?"

Grumbling at her casual remark about my near-death experience, I tugged the still-quivering blade from the wood. "You shouldn't try to kill someone without knowing who it is first."

"My motto is maim first, ask questions later." She took in

my outfit with a satisfied smirk, and I couldn't help the accompanying blush. "Well, well, well. Someone cleans up nicely."

"Oh stop, this is all your fault." I dropped the knife on her desk with a clatter and studied her face. She looked more tired than usual, the lines around her eyes deeper. "Who was on the phone?"

A fleeting look of resignation passed over her features. "What'd you hear?"

I sat across from her. "Enough to know something's changed. I wasn't trying to listen, I just didn't want to interrupt."

She waved a hand dismissively. "No need to fret, my pet. I'll figure it out."

"Frankie, what happened?"

Leaning back in her chair—which protested with a loud, drawn-out groan—she kicked her boots onto the desk. She was trying hard not to show the worry that was all too evident in her gaze. "The collection date's been moved up."

"To when?"

"Three weeks sooner."

Shock surged through me, and I jerked my head back as if I'd been slapped. "What? But we won't earn enough from the massages in a week."

"I know, kid, I know." Shaking out a cigarette from the box on her desk, she lit it and took a deep drag before exhaling. "Don't worry. I'll figure it out. You know I always do."

An uneasy feeling crept into the pit of my stomach. Smoking and Frankie went hand in hand like seagrass and krill jam, but never in her office. An ashtray lay within reach, and it was full of fresh ashes. She kept the gym smoke-free, which meant this situation was way more serious than she was letting on.

There was an easy way to fix our problem, but it meant letting the land world know exactly what I was. Possibly even *who* I was. My throat constricted, stealing the oxygen from my lungs.

Was I ready to out myself like that? To put my sister in danger again?

Without lowering her boots, Frankie leaned forward and plucked a picture frame off her desk. She flipped it around to show me, a grin on her face. "Remember that day? You two were so green to bein' landlubbers."

I knew the picture like the back of my hand. It was the three of us—Frankie, Marissa, and me—getting ready to take the Metro for the first time.

Well, technically it was our second, but I'd been too filled with fear to appreciate the first time. And Frankie had practically grown up on them.

The happy grins on our faces were stupidly contagious, but I'd gripped Marissa's hand like she was about to disappear. I would never forget that first experience with Frankie since it was the closest I'd come to feeling like I was swimming through the ocean waves again.

I glanced at my boss, who studied the photo with a loving expression. She was like a mother to us, though she'd hate for me to say it. Maybe just an older sister.

Maybe I was feeling overly confident after the date, but I had to do this for her. For all of us.

"I'll do it."

"Do what?" She took another drag of her cigarette and rubbed her thumb across a smudge on the picture frame.

"Fight."

Her thumb stilled on the glass, and she slowly blew out the smoke in thick rings. "Don't say shit like that unless you're serious."

"I am serious. This is my home thanks to you. Thanks to your unwavering generosity. I owe you this much."

She set the frame down and met my determined gaze. "Let's get one thing straight. You don't owe me nothin', girl. You've worked your ass off here. I probably owe *you*."

I smiled. "Yeah, probably. But I'm serious. I'll do it."

Her eyes narrowed as she studied me, probably trying to figure out if I was actually being serious. Finally, she dropped her feet to the ground and put out the cigarette.

"Okay, then. I ain't above takin' your charity. But we'll set it up right, kid. Only one fight, I promise." Her voice grew more animated as she continued. "We'll get the big names in here to watch and ramp up excitement, charge at the door, take a percentage of any bets."

As I listened to her rattle on with a tense smile plastered on my face, my thoughts tumbled as tumultuously as an ocean storm. It was obvious she'd thought about this before—a lot.

Terror and guilt vied for my attention, both of which had a death grip on my stomach. One told me to flee before it was too late while the other demanded I protect my home and family.

Was I doing the right thing? Would Frankie protect me and Marissa if things went sour?

Could she even protect us?

CHAPTER 19

Dominic

After the limousine pulled away from Subliminal, Dominic leaned back against the leather seat and messaged Rin and Keiko to meet him for the job. His grip tightened on the phone, his fury growing with every passing moment.

Of all the days for something to go wrong.

And it had gone very wrong. Ichiro would never call him to step in like this unless it was serious. Not because the old man valued Dominic's free time, but because he hated admitting he needed his bastard grandson to clean up a mess.

The good news was it further proved that Dominic was the best choice to take over the Sato empire. His dragon was one of the fiercest, most lethal spirits since Ichiro's, possibly even rivaling that vicious old beast. Naming anyone else would make his grandfather look like a fool, and a fool he was not.

Dominic let the satisfaction of that thought curl around his anger until the emotion loosened its vise-like hold. He needed a clear mind for what he was about to do.

When the limousine stopped outside a warehouse not far

from the National Arboretum, Dominic opened the door and stepped out without waiting for Samson.

His driver met him beside the car's door. "Shall I come back later, sir?"

"No, this won't take long." He strode to the trunk and popped it open. A treasure trove of weapons waited within—guns, knives, explosives, and more.

A familiar figure slipped out of the surrounding darkness, his dark eyes tinged with red. Rin's dragon was ready and waiting. "Keiko's getting into place."

They had done enough jobs together over the years that each knew their roles without being told. In silence, the two men strapped a few extra knives and guns to their bodies as a precaution, but their real weapons were imprinted on their skin forever.

Satisfied with their selections, Dominic closed the trunk, and Rin followed him toward the building where the transaction and subsequent fuck-up had occurred. They strode into the warehouse as if they owned the place.

Technically, Dominic did own it by way of his grandfather and the family business. This was his turf, and he would defend it head-on.

Their footsteps echoed throughout the vast building until they reached the center of an open space between shipping containers where Kenzo knelt. Six armed men surrounded him in a wide circle, while a man wearing a dark hoodie covering his face stood behind him, holding a Desert Eagle to Kenzo's head.

At that distance, a bullet might prove lethal to a dragon, especially one as weak as Kenzo's.

His cousin's right eye was swollen and bruised, and a gag kept him from saying anything stupid. His trembling hands were zip-tied in front of him. The tie was similar to a standard, plastic zip tie, but this one was capable of suppressing his dragon's spirit. Without a doubt, a bullet would be fatal.

Ichiro hadn't given Dominic any details other than this was a transaction gone awry, but he should have known his cousin would be involved in this big of a fuck up. When would the old man learn? Kenzo was never going to change, and why would he? Everything in his entitled life came free.

Approaching the group with a casual swagger, Dominic surveyed the half dozen men surrounding them before smirking. "Did my invite get lost in the mail?"

"Nah, we don't usually invite your type to our parties." The man holding the gun shrugged and tilted his head up, revealing his face. "Maybe next time, though, eh, dragon?"

Black hair, dark eyes, and a distinctive goatee identified him as Francisco Jaurez, also known as Paco and the ruthless leader of the Nightstalkers Pack. Wolf shifters didn't live in cities often, but it wasn't completely unheard of, particularly in bigger cities where it was easier to hide among such a large, non-Gifted population.

Like the Sato empire, the Nightstalkers worked together as a family unit, though their reach in the city's sordid underbelly wasn't nearly as widespread as the Satos. They were up-and-comers, constantly pushing the boundaries to try to take over more of the Sato share.

Too bad for them, Dominic was more than prepared to defend his territory, and tonight, his dragon had a thirst for blood.

"What are we doing here, boys?" He spread his arms, gesturing to the men surrounding them. "You trying to get yourselves killed?"

Paco laughed and pressed his gun harder against the back of Kenzo's head. "Only one person is looking to get himself killed today. Your boy's trying to pull a fast one on us."

Dominic's lip curled in distaste. "Please, Paco, you know me better than that. Kenzo's not my boy. Unfortunately for us both, I can't let you kill him. Maybe next time."

Over the gag, his cousin glared daggers at him. The idiot was too stupid to live much longer. Someone would take care of the issue, just not today.

"Not much you can do about it, homie." Paco grinned, displaying glittery bling across his teeth. Kenzo would fit right in with these fools. "If you hadn't noticed, you're outnumbered. I knew you'd turn up eventually, seeing how tight Ichiro's leash is, so I brought my friends to have some fun."

Beside Dominic, Rin cracked his neck. "You sure about that, *homie*?"

Paco's smile faltered. He glanced at one of his men and tilted his head.

Keeping his gun raised, the man took a few steps toward a stack of containers and called something out in Spanish. They waited.

Nothing but glorious silence.

As the armed men exchanged wary glances, a shadow dripped down the side of the closest wall of shipping containers. The pool of darkness slithered along the ground, undetected by the wolves. Ironic that a group calling themselves Nightstalkers would be so oblivious to the danger in their midst.

The shadow slipped behind one of the wolves and pulled itself upright, coalescing into a tiny female form dressed in black from head to toe. The figure slid her dagger under the man's chin, and his eyes flew open with surprise.

Her fangs were covered in crimson as she grinned. "Am I late?"

Before he could react, she drew the blade across his throat. Blood rained down his front as he fell to the ground, shock etched onto his face.

Paco aimed his gun at Keiko. "You."

She pointed at herself. "Me?"

"You're not real," he stammered.

Her eyes opened wide behind her mask. "That's news to me."

To most of the Gifted community, Keiko was known simply as Death. She left few survivors to tell the tale of her slaughter, so her existence had become like a bogeyman, a nightmare to scare subordinates into submission and enemies into surrendering.

No one outside the Sato family knew her true identity, and those within the family could be counted on one hand. Anyone else who happened to find out quickly forgot again—with the help of a witch they had on staff—or they met their maker.

Keiko wasn't a dragon. She was something more rare than a siren and much more lethal than any of them, including Dominic.

Paco paled, likely realizing he wouldn't leave this room alive. None of his men would. Despite that realization, he decided to fight back.

Except she was gone before he even pulled the trigger. The bullet slammed into a shipping container and all hell broke loose.

As Paco's men raised their guns or shifted into their wolf

forms with resounding cracks as their bones reformed, Dominic unleashed his dragon. The beast's echoing roars gained in volume as it emerged from his skin like a fiery wraith.

His back smoldered red hot, but it was a feeling he'd long since learned to accept and embrace. The pain kept him focused.

As Death danced from guard to guard, dispatching each with precision and grace that always turned Dominic's blood cold, Rin scooped Kenzo up under his arm and dragged him out of the fray.

All this bloodshed for that waste of space.

Dominic stepped in front of Paco. The Nightstalkers' alpha pulled the trigger again and again, but each bullet bounced off his dragon-hardened skin, flattened by the impact. When the clip was empty, Paco met his gaze.

He expected to see fear in the man's eyes, not angry determination.

Bones cracked and popped as Paco shifted into his other form, his eyes glowing with an otherworldly intensity and his clothes shredding around him. His wolf was massive, coming up to Dominic's waist, and his inky black coat bristled.

He knew he was going to die, but he would fight to the end. The least Dominic could do was give him a worthy death.

Unbuttoning his shirt, he removed it and his shoes, not wanting either to restrict or hinder his movements. His slacks were loose enough to maneuver in.

The air carried a sense of impending doom as they circled each other, Dominic's muscles tensing with each step. Years of training for these exact circumstances had honed his reflexes, but fighting a man prepared to die was never easy.

Paco lunged forward with blinding speed.

Letting his instincts take over, Dominic knocked the wolf to the side and countered with a series of sharp kicks and punches, each strike calculated for precision. His hits landed, but the wolf's resilience was astonishing. He shrugged off blows that would have dropped any lesser opponent.

As they circled each other again, Dominic noticed a pattern in the wolf's attacks. The beast's moves were becoming more predictable, and he seized an opportunity.

With a lightning-quick jab to the wolf's solar plexus followed by a powerful roundhouse kick, he sent the alpha sprawling across the warehouse floor.

But Paco wasn't finished yet. He growled and leaped to his feet before launching himself at Dominic like a relentless predator.

As Dominic ducked under the lunge, he swiped his claws upward.

The wolf crashed to the ground with a soul-shattering whine. Shifting back to his human form, Paco collapsed onto his knees. He held a hand to his stomach as if he could stop his intestines from spilling out.

"Tell Ichiro...we know what he's doing." Each word was a struggle. He coughed, and blood bubbled out of his mouth. "We won't let him...turn us into...his slaves."

Dominic had no idea what he was referring to. "Explain."

"The pyrocrystals..." Paco fell onto his side and released his entrails.

The hair on the back of Dominic's neck raised. "What about the crystals?"

"Ask...Kenzo..." The man exhaled for the last time.

Whatever Dominic was about to learn, he knew he wasn't going to like it.

After retrieving his shirt and shoes, he left the carnage behind him and strode from the warehouse. Outside, he found Rin and Kenzo standing beside the limousine.

Kenzo rubbed his chafed wrists. "You—"

Dominic's hand wrapped around his cousin's throat, cutting his words and air supply off. "Tell me about the crystals."

Kenzo's eyes bulged out of his head as he yanked at Dominic's arm. He loosened his grip just enough to let the kid speak. "What do you—"

Tightening his grip again, he gave Kenzo a rough shake. "Don't be even more stupid than you already are. How is Ichiro involved?"

This time, he dropped Kenzo completely.

The idiot nearly fell over, and he coughed and gasped as if he'd been tortured for hours. He glared at Dominic. "Ichiro knows everything. It was his idea. Who else has the means to start something like this?"

"Jesus fucking Christ," Rin muttered.

So Ichiro had been aware of Kenzo's little side project when they visited the pawnshop. Not only aware, but if his cousin was correct, the old man was the mastermind behind it all. He was knowingly creating addicts and doing it to control them.

He knew his grandfather was capable of atrocious acts of violence, but this?

This was the worst by far.

Had Dominic killed the wrong man tonight?

Disgust roiled within his stomach, thick and full of acid. Pyrocrystals were far too dangerous for non-dragons to use. The confrontation at the pawnshop was proof of that.

A shadow solidified beside him, and Keiko opened her

palm, revealing a cluster of red crystals. "The wolves were trying to steal a container filled with them."

He took the pyrocrystals from her and crushed them in his fist, letting the crimson dust scatter in the night air. Fury seethed beneath his skin as he considered the unexpected turn of events that evening.

Ichiro had hidden this from him for months. Yet tonight, he demanded Dominic step in, knowing he would discover his grandfather's secret. He wanted Dominic to know, which meant the old man was confident no one would be able to interfere, not even the Red Dragon.

Except, once again, Ichiro had underestimated the monster he had created.

"What do you want me to do with Kenzo?" Rin asked.

Samson met Dominic at the limousine's door and handed him a towel. He wiped the blood from his hands and said, "Let him find his own way home."

"And the crystals?" Keiko asked, her features still masked.

Resting a hand on the door, he turned to stare at the building.

Over the years, Dominic had sometimes questioned his place within the family, not quite sure he wanted to become head of the Sato empire after Ichiro. It wasn't that he was against the immoral endeavors of their various enterprises—until now—but he wanted to be known for a higher purpose than that. He'd once thought fighting in the ring was his true purpose.

Now, he knew he had no choice. No one else would be willing or able to put a stop to this madness. Not when money and power were at stake, and certainly not when Ichiro Sato was involved.

Dominic needed to make a statement. Something that would let Ichiro know he wouldn't stand for this level of depravity.

He clenched his jaw until something cracked. "Burn it to the ground."

CHAPTER 20

Bree

Word about the upcoming fight had gotten around the gym, and talk of a "mystery" fighter stirred the excitement into a frenzy that was sure to alert the authorities. Sure to alert them had Frankie not had ironclad charms protecting the place, that is.

But not literal iron, seeing how she was fae. The metal could be downright lethal to her kind.

Iron properties aside, I was pretty sure she had friends on the force who made a pretty penny with bets on fight nights.

My boss scheduled the event for Friday night, right before the debt was due, to give us the most amount of time to prepare and train. I'd argued that the date was cutting it way too close. All sorts of things could happen over the next few days that might set us back, which we absolutely couldn't do with potential homelessness looming over our heads.

But she'd waved away my worries as if they were nothing more than pesky piranhas. She loved the adrenaline rush that came with a tight deadline.

That made one of us.

As I wound my way past groups of sweaty gym members and weight benches, Marissa's laugh by the front door caught my attention. I paused to watch her in action. She rested a delicate hand on some gym member's arm, leaning into him as she dazzled him with her smile. Then she handed him a flyer announcing the fight.

I guess that made two of us who loved the adrenaline rush.

At least the flyer would disintegrate once it left the gym thanks to a fae spell. Shaking my head in amusement, I continued toward the basement door and slipped inside our semi-underground sanctuary.

I wished I could be as carefree as she was. Maybe I would be someday, once Marissa was finished with school and able to stand on her own two feet. If that day ever came.

When I'd told her about the upcoming fight, my sister had jumped in to help without hesitation. She'd always wanted me to compete, not because she was proud of me but because she thought it would bring fame and fortune—for her.

Okay, that might have been too harsh.

She was proud of me, but she also wanted fame and fortune. Who could blame her? Most people seemed to want the same. As usual, I was the odd fish out.

We didn't even know who I would fight against yet. Frankie was collecting names, and she didn't want to rush the decision. Whoever it was, they needed to be among the best Subliminal had to offer to draw the biggest crowd possible. We'd even consider someone who hadn't fought at our gym if word spread far and fast enough.

After feeding Finley some canned crab meat—yes, he usually ate better than I did—I took a quick shower before curling up on the corner of my bed. I grabbed the book I'd started the night before and cracked it open. I'd have the next hour all to myself to read in peace and quiet.

Only three pages in, my phone buzzed next to my leg. I glanced at it briefly, expecting a junk mail notification or something, and returned my attention to the book.

Then my brain caught up with what I'd read on the screen.

I snatched the phone up too quickly, fumbling it between my hands before I caught it and stared at the screen. My smile grew as I read the message again: *Not kissing those delectable lips for two days is unacceptable.*

Yes, somehow two days had passed since I'd last seen Dominic. In person, that is. I saw him every night in my dreams and just as often in my daydreams while cleaning. We'd both gotten caught up in our respective responsibilities, but I agreed with him completely—two days was too long.

A sharp knock came from the back door leading up to the street level.

I yelped and nearly dropped my phone again. Other than Marissa and me, no one ever used that door. No one could because Frankie had cast a glamour to hide it.

Finley chirped within his aquarium. A bubble floated out of his mouth as he swayed sleepily among the seaweed, his belly nice and full. He tilted his head to the side with an expression that said he was just as confused as I was.

My heart thudded wildly. I thought I'd been overly paranoid lately, thinking my father had finally found us. But maybe I wasn't so paranoid after all.

I slipped off my bed and over to the wall, sliding closer to the door and holding a finger up to my lips to keep Finley quiet. There was no real reason to be sneaky. Without windows, no one could see I was home. But my yelp might have given me away.

The knock came again, and I jumped, pressing a hand to my chest. This was getting ridiculous. I could take care of myself.

Squaring my shoulders, I grabbed the closest thing that could act as a weapon and yanked open the door, ready to defend myself.

A man's back was to me as he was about to head up the stairs. He turned around, one foot on the steps, and my brain practically melted.

Dominic.

Today, he wore something completely unexpected—black jeans that hugged his sculpted thighs and a black leather jacket over a white t-shirt that stretched tight across his pecs. A black helmet with the Sato's fire dragon family crest painted across it was tucked under his arm.

A slight scruff covered his chin, the shadow effect accentuating his strong jaw, and his black hair was disheveled in a super sexy way that made me want to run my fingers through it.

Tides, he was so freaking beautiful.

"Nic? What are you doing here?"

"So you are home." His deep amber gaze dipped to the object I gripped tight, and he grinned. "Expecting rain?

Hastily, I set the umbrella against the wall and slipped on some ratty sneakers I kept near the door. I stepped outside and closed the door, not wanting him to witness the mess that was living with Marissa. "Wait, how'd you see this door?"

His eyes swept over my body, glinting with a hint of humor. "The magic only keeps the non-Gifted from seeing it."

Too late, I realized what I was wearing. Leggings and a

faded, oversized shirt weren't exactly what I'd want him to see me in. Or anyone, for that matter.

I tucked my wet hair behind my ears, trying to hide my discomfort but probably making it more obvious. Such was my luck. "Can I help you with something?"

"I want to take you somewhere," he said and held out his hand.

Caught off guard, I simply stared at his hand. "Right now?"

He slipped his palm into mine. His touch spread warmth through my body like an inferno as he pulled me toward the stairs. "Trust me. You'll love it."

I was too shocked to do anything but follow him until we reached the street level, where he plopped the helmet on my head. His intense gaze roved over my face as he buckled it into place.

Was he...*smoldering* at me?

"What are you—"

I stopped when I saw the motorcycle, adorned with a matching dragon crest painted along its side. I'd never ridden on one before, but after reading more than a few books involving them, I'd added the experience to my bucket list. They seemed dangerous in an adventurous and fun way.

Sadly, I'd never known anyone who had a motorcycle before today. I guess times were a-changing.

He grabbed the other helmet and tugged it onto his head then swung a leg over the bike. He started it up and revved the engine before facing me. "Get on."

"Nic, wait, I'm not even dressed in real clothes, like going out in public clothes," I gestured to myself, panicking slightly, " and, uh, I've got stuff—"

"You don't need to impress me, Bree. I happen to find you

uncomfortably sexy right now." His gaze captured mine as he adjusted the front of his jeans, proving his point.

Heat flushed across my cheeks as I stood there, dumbfounded. My heart and head were at war with one another. I wanted nothing more than to slide on that bike behind him, feeling his warmth between my thighs, a thought that had me gulping.

Except this kind of behavior was reckless. I had to get back to my job soon, and I hardly knew Dominic. I mean, I knew quite a bit about him from my years watching him fight and my recent internet stalking.

But I didn't really *know* him, and everything I'd read practically screamed to stay far, *far* away from him.

"When was the last time you did something for yourself?" His words cut to my core and snatched my breath away. His smirk taunted me, knowing he'd struck a nerve. "Live a little. Now, get on."

He was right. I never did anything for myself besides read, and that was only when I had breaks. I mean, sure, I'd let him pamper me before our date, but that was because I'd been kidnapped and forced to enjoy it.

Stop overthinking it, Bree!

Before I could dart away faster than a spooked clownfish, I slung my leg over the bike behind him and wrapped my arms around his waist. It was like holding onto a... Well, a dragon. The man was all hard muscle and delightfully rigid planes.

A rumble passed through his body into mine, teasing every nerve. "I'd be lying if I said I didn't want you gripping a little lower. Hold on tight, beautiful."

He revved the engine again and the tires squealed against the asphalt before we shot forward. With a precision that demonstrated his obvious experience but did little to calm my racing pulse, he wove around cars and dodged pedestrians, rarely slowing down.

My heart pounded with every wild second, and on more than one occasion, I squeezed my eyes shut and prayed for mercy. But as we flew through the streets of D.C., the fear slowly melted into something else—exhilaration.

If I thought riding the Metro trains was the closest sensation to swimming, it was nothing compared to the rush of wind through my hair and tugging at my clothes. I had the wildest urge to let go of his waist and raise my arms toward the sky.

But I didn't. Not that I was afraid, necessarily. Gifted types were much stronger than typical humans, and we healed faster too.

No, I just didn't want to let Dominic go. I leaned into his warmth and smiled.

We followed a winding road away from the bustling city streets, where the trees towered toward the sky and formed leafy archways over our heads. In my decade of living on land, I'd never once explored this far away from home. While I didn't regret it, I realized how much I'd been missing out on.

He slowed, and I peeked around him to see why we were stopping. Only we didn't stop. He turned off the main road onto a barely visible path leading through the trees and then revved the engine. We soared through a sea of green, bushes and overhanging branches trying to impede our way.

When he finally slowed again and stopped, I leaned around his shoulders and gasped.

CHAPTER 21

Bree

The most magnificent sight sprawled out before us. I slid off the bike and removed my helmet, leaving it on the seat before I climbed up onto a large rock to see better.

We had parked between trees near the edge of a river. The water fell over a series of steep, jagged rocks and created beautifully cascading waterfalls. Roaring as they stretched across the expanse, the falls sent spray up into the air and created rainbows everywhere I looked.

I breathed in deeply, smiling. The water smelled so much fresher here than in the city, which wasn't surprising considering how far upstream we must have been.

On the opposite side of the river, people gathered along rocks and wooden decks overlooking the falls. They looked like crawling ants from this distance.

"What is this place?"

"Great Falls," Dominic said, his voice deeper than usual.

As I tore my gaze away from the scenery to check on him, the wind whipped my hair across my face.

He still sat on his bike, but his eyes blazed with carnal

hunger. He removed his helmet and let it drop to the ground. "You have never looked more like a goddess than you do right now. Come here."

This time, I didn't hesitate to obey his command. I stepped down from the rock and approached him.

With a low growl, he drew me onto his lap, facing him. He lowered his head to my throat and dragged his nose up my skin. His lips brushed against me softly, and goosebumps rose across my entire body.

Oh, sweet pearl of Tethys.

I couldn't believe this was happening, that he wanted me this way. I'd dreamed of something like this happening with him years ago, but I'd long since given up those fantasies until two days ago.

After our steamy kiss on the National Mall, those fantasies reignited like fireworks on the fourth of July. And despite his promise to make up for the interruption that night, I'd assumed that date was a one-time deal, especially since I hadn't seen him since.

"You have no idea what you do to me, do you?" His voice was low and dangerous, and he grazed his teeth across the sensitive skin of my neck.

I tilted my head to the side, granting him better access, and moved my hands up his chest to grip his jacket. My body was on fire with need. "Oh, I have an idea."

His hands grasped my thighs and squeezed tight.

Gasping as his grip did wild things to my insides, I wrapped my arms around the back of his neck and tugged his face to mine. I needed more from him, much more. Our lips touched, and lightning struck within me.

His hands moved to my waist, slipping underneath my shirt to touch my bare skin.

I moaned against him, his rock-hard length pressing into me through his jeans. Loving the way he felt, loving the way *I* felt when he touched me, I still wanted more. There was no doubt in my mind where this was headed, and I was more than ready.

Except...

Despite the wondrous feelings, my hesitant thoughts threatened to halt everything. Dominic ignited something within me, an almost primal craving. But I knew his reputation.

He might say everything right, make me feel special and desired, but actions spoke louder than words. This could be just another conquest for him. Nothing more than a tick on a scoresheet. He might get what he wanted and then move on, as he always did.

But for some insane reason, I didn't care.

Not truly. I wanted to throw caution to the wind for the once-in-a-lifetime chance of seeing and touching more of him. I longed to know what it felt like to be with the Red Dragon so intimately, even if it was over after today.

I didn't know how long this...*thing* with Dominic would last, if at all, but I was determined to enjoy this moment to its fullest.

Today would be for me.

Without breaking the kiss, I pushed his jacket off his shoulders and down his arms.

He tossed it to the side, and I wasted no time slipping my hands beneath his shirt. We pulled apart long enough to get the shirt over his head, and I stared in wonder at his perfectly sculpted, bronze body, running my fingertips across his smooth chest.

It was one thing to touch him while pretending to be a masseuse, and a whole other thing to touch him like this, to know his skin was hot because of me. The urge to be skin-to-skin became unbearable.

Grabbing the hem of my shirt, I yanked it over my head and dropped it.

His gaze dipped to my confined breasts, rising and falling with my ragged breaths, and his pupils constricted. His palms, rough with callouses, slid up my back to unclasp my bra.

Thank Tethys, I'd opted for my newest—though still humble and simple—bra rather than one of the ratty old ones. I slid the straps down my arms, watching for his reaction as I removed the bra completely.

Crimson flared to life within his irises, and his erection pulsed beneath me. He ran his hands up my sides to cup each breast in his palms.

It was all I could do not to moan again, so I bit my lip to hold it in.

With a deep growl, he reached up and dragged his thumb across my bottom lip, tugging it free of my teeth. "No, don't you dare hold back. You are a goddess, Bree. Every pleasure in this world should be yours."

I stared at him, breathless. Not that I had many men to compare Dominic to besides book boyfriends, but no man had ever spoken to me like that before. No man outside my fantasies, anyway. "You say that to all your conquests?"

"No." He narrowed his gaze. Not in anger but in pure, unbridled desire. "I've only met one goddess—you. And you are far from a conquest."

Talk about making my panties drop.

Not literally, of course, considering how we were sitting.

As if sharing that thought, he gently pushed me back against the handlebars and lifted my hips. As he pulled my leggings and underwear down and off my legs, his hungry gaze roved over every naked inch of me.

Despite the day's warmth, I shivered, though I was far from cold. I might not have been a virgin, but I rarely exposed myself like this to a man, so fully. I felt vulnerable in a weirdly sexy way.

Slowly, he slid his hands up my legs, spreading them wide before him. As he drank in the sight between my legs, he let out a tortured groan and squeezed my thighs.

The sound rumbled through me, teasing my core into a frenzy. Unable to restrain myself, I gasped and arched my back, thrusting my breasts upward.

He dipped his head to my breast, taking my nipple into his hot mouth and sucking hard.

A cry of startled pleasure escaped my lips. My few sexual experiences had always been on a bed in a darkened room. They'd never included much more than a quick make-out session followed by even quicker sex. Fun but fast, and very little in the way of groping and foreplay.

This slow exploration was new and oh so deliciously excruciating, reminding me of steamy romance books I'd read. I was pleasantly surprised to find how much I liked it happening to me. I reached between us to unbutton his jeans.

Except his hand grabbed mine, stopping me. He released my nipple with a pop and secured both my hands in one strong grip above my head.

In a breathy daze, I blinked at him, confused and needing more.

His lips tilted up into a wicked smirk. "Let me worship you."

Before I could ask what that meant, he slid his free hand between my legs and slipped a finger inside me. "Fuck. You're already so wet for me, Bree."

I moaned, loving the sensations he provoked with each stroke. His touch was pure ecstasy, and I was high as a kite. I gripped my hands together above my head, unable to do much else with them restrained in this way, and rocked against his palm between my legs.

He slid another finger inside and moved his hand faster. Diving deeper, his fingers curled with each thrust while his thumb swirled against my clit.

His amber gaze never left mine, but try as I might, I couldn't keep my eyes open. My eyelids fluttered shut, and I dropped my head back against the bike, ecstasy flowing through my veins like a drug.

He was ruining me in the best way imaginable.

"Nic..." My breaths came out faster and shallower. The promised release built as I whimpered and rocked, and I feared for a brief moment that I might tip the entire bike over.

Then suddenly, my world exploded.

I cried out as I climaxed, squeezing my thighs against him, my back arching off the bike. My body shuddered with each pleasurable wave crashing through me.

When I finally slumped back against the bike, panting heavily, Dominic released my hands and slid his fingers out. His gaze was still fixed on mine as he raised his hand to his mouth and licked the fingers that were inside me as if devouring his favorite meal.

The move was so erotic and nothing I'd ever expected to enjoy watching. I was sure it had a lot to do with the man doing it. Even though I'd just orgasmed, my body throbbed with the need for more.

He pressed a soft kiss to my shoulder. "You are unbelievable."

"Me?" Chucking, I ran my fingers through his dark hair. The strands were as silky as I expected. "You did all the work."

He kissed his way up my neck to my jaw. "Very few women let themselves go the way you just did."

Heat rose in my cheeks, and my fingers stilled in his hair. "What do you mean?"

Dominic ran his thumb across my lips, tempting me to capture it in my mouth. "The noises you made. It was all I could do to hold back until you came."

Covering my face with my hands, I laughed softly. "Oh, my good gravy."

He pulled my hands away. "I loved every fucking sound." To prove his point, he rocked his hips forward against my still-sensitive core, his hard length rubbing me through his jeans.

I gasped as the friction sent aftershocks shooting through my body. I was more than willing to go again, only this time I wanted him completely.

But once again, he stopped me as I reached for his jeans.

"Today was just for you, my goddess." He grabbed my leggings and underwear from the seat behind him. After gently slipping each of my legs inside, he slid them up and over my hips. His gaze captured mine before dipping to my swollen lips. "But I promise you this: you'll be screaming my name until your throat is raw, every time I fuck you."

Well, that settled it—I was in big trouble.

Because whatever my future held, I knew Dominic would be part of it.

CHAPTER 22

Bree

As the sun dipped toward the horizon, I walked home from the grocery store, carrying two paper bags and humming a tune from my childhood. A bubble of excitement danced in my stomach, and I smiled, not even caring who might think I was a madwoman.

A few days had passed since our steamy motorcycle ride, and Dominic's work responsibilities—a job I tried not to think about all that much—kept him too busy to see me in person. I'd worried that my worst fears had come true, that I was a one-time conquest and nothing more.

Except he'd squashed those fears quickly and continued to stomp them down every chance he got.

After looking both ways to make sure the road was clear, I stepped off the sidewalk and crossed the street.

Much to Marissa's delight and Frankie's annoyance, the gym was filled with a rainbow of tulips, my favorite flower. All thanks to the numerous bouquets he'd sent since discovering that tidbit about me on Sunday. He claimed he couldn't make up his mind which one I'd like best, so he ordered them all.

Logic didn't always prevail when your bank account ended in that many zeroes.

As if that weren't sweet enough—yet also somewhat crazy—I'd never been on my phone so much over the past ten years as I did just in just the past three days. We were like giddy grade schoolers, sending texts and calling each other every spare moment we had.

His last text in particular played on constant repeat in my thoughts and fueled my fantasies: *I'm going crazy with the need to taste you again.*

That made two of us.

His walls had come crumbling down, showing me a deeper side than I ever expected him to have and surprising me at every turn. I loved getting to know the man hidden beneath that heartless, playboy mask he wore.

He was caring and kind, sophisticated, and so freaking sexy. My body warmed as I walked, once again dreaming of his hands on my skin, exploring the most sensitive parts of me as the waterfalls crashed behind us.

Romantic didn't come close.

Every moment of getting to know him had been amazing, and I had never been this happy in my entire life.

How had I gotten so lucky to be living my very own fairytale?

I adjusted one of the grocery bags against my side. They weren't too heavy, but several cans were poking me in the gut. Thankfully, the gym was only a few more blocks away.

I hadn't told Dominic about my role in the upcoming fight yet, not necessarily because I was trying to keep it from him, but the topic never seemed to come up. When I was on the phone with him late at night, all my worries and concerns floated away. Forgotten.

It wasn't until I was about to fall asleep that I would remember. I couldn't just text him about something as big as that, but I didn't want to tell him over the phone either.

To be honest, I wasn't sure how he would feel about me fighting, considering how dangerous the matches were. So I decided it was a discussion best had in person. I just didn't know when or if I'd get the chance before Friday.

The sun sank below the horizon, and long shadows stretched farther across the sidewalk, ready to devour everything in darkness. As a Gifted person in the city, walking alone at night didn't scare me. I could hold my own against regular humans, and most likely anyone else too.

But tonight, something felt different.

I glanced behind me, my skin crawling with unease. Nothing appeared out of the ordinary—car headlights had flicked on and the throng of pedestrians had thinned as rush hour wrapped up. Those out now were looking for food, drinks, or a gym, completely absorbed in their own bubbles.

Still, my scalp prickled with the distinct feeling of being watched.

Turning back around, I increased my speed until an older man with dark grey hair and tanned skin stopped a few feet in front of me. He had on casual clothes and looked like any ordinary person on the street...

Until I saw his eyes.

That familiar, deep aqua gaze penetrated down to my soul. The knowledge of his presence here latched around my lungs, squeezing painfully.

Oh, schnitzel.

Demetrius, the captain of my father's guard, stepped closer with his hands raised. "Princess Gabrielle, please—"

"Stay away from me!" My outburst surprised even me, and I tripped over the uneven sidewalk. The side of one of my paper bags ripped, sending groceries tumbling in every direction.

The few people around us cast nervous glances in our direction but continued on their way as soon as I scrambled to grab anything headed for the street. Clearly, I wasn't being attacked if I was worried about wayward vegetables.

I didn't even notice Demetrius getting closer until he handed me a can of mushroom soup.

"Sending you is low, even for him." I swiped the can from his hand. "I'm not going back. He doesn't own me *or* Marissa."

His smile was sad as he helped me collect the rest of my groceries, placing everything into one way-too-full bag. "King Proteus didn't send me to bring you home."

I scooped up the bag with both arms, hoping it would hold the rest of the way. "I'm not a child anymore, Demetri. Nor am I a fool."

He chuckled and followed as I headed for home again. "No, you are neither of those things, that is true. But it is also true that I am not lying."

We stopped at a red light, and I cast a wary glance at him. "Then why are you here?"

His eyebrows drew together in an expression I couldn't quite read. "To warn you to stay away."

I stared at him in complete bewilderment. Never in my wildest dreams had I expected that response. Relief was short-lived, however, as suspicion crept in. My father warning me to stay away was as likely as a dolphin growing a horn.

Demetrius nudged my arm, snapping me out of it enough to cross the street while we had the green light.

"I don't understand," I said plainly.

"There is some trouble brewing back home." His words were carefully chosen. Only two buildings away from the gym, he stopped me and glanced up and down the street. "He wishes for you both to remain safe from any harm."

Goosebumps prickled across my skin. "What trouble?"

"The details are not important. What's important is that you listen and obey."

I couldn't help it, I laughed.

His startled gaze fell on me before he smiled ruefully, and deep crinkles formed beside his eyes. "Yes, I see the humor. If not to him, then listen to me, little Ree."

My heart constricted, twisting until tears formed in my eyes. This man had been more of a father to me than my own. He'd been by my side since my birth, and he was there to patch the pieces of my heart back together when my mother died. Besides my sister, he was the only other person alive allowed to call me by that name.

And it was only because of him that I was able to escape with Marissa all those years ago.

I sighed. "Fine. I can only assume that whatever this trouble is isn't as bad as you're making it out to be if he let you leave his side."

His smile drooped, but I didn't get a chance to ask about the change in his expression.

Loud voices erupted behind me, and I spun around, still on edge. A group of gym members had burst out of Subliminal, laughing and talking excitedly. I chuckled and turned to ask Demetrius if he wanted to see where we'd ended up.

Except he was gone.

IN A RARE TURN OF EVENTS, MY SISTER WAS HOME when I arrived. She sat on her cot with one leg pulled up and her chin propped on her knee while scrolling through her phone. But in true Marissa fashion, she didn't offer to help me put any of our groceries away.

To be fair, I'd already put the cold stuff in the office fridge. There wasn't much left to set on our makeshift kitchen cabinet, which was just a wobbly plastic bookshelf held together with duct tape.

I didn't want to scare her by telling her about seeing Demetrius, but my nerves were still amped up from his unexpected visit. I needed to get some of that energy out, which meant training, as I'd done every night this week.

"Want to practice with me?"

"Pass." Her eyes never left her phone.

I placed the last box of microwavable macaroni and cheese cups on a shelf. "Don't you need to stay fit for massages, though?"

"I'm sure non-Gifted people do," she said, then laughed at something on her phone.

I folded up the paper bag and tucked it behind the shelf. "What's so funny?"

This time, her gaze lifted to mine. She raised an eyebrow. "What's wrong with you?"

"Well, that's rude." Not that she was wrong. Normally, I didn't try to talk to her when she was on her phone. It was like talking to a volcano: either she ignored me or exploded in a fit of rage. Humans said it was a red-headed thing, and I tended to believe them.

But you couldn't just say stuff like that out loud.

I grabbed a tuna can and pulled the tab to open it.

Immediately, Finley popped out from wherever he was hiding amid his tank's seaweed and swam to the aquarium's surface. His eager eyes fell on the can.

"Sorry, buddy." I set the can on the table near his tank. He clambered down and started munching away. Only a drop of water ended up on the table beside him before he dried himself with magic. "Next time let Marissa know you're this hungry if I'm not back yet."

"She's such a worrier, isn't she?" She winked at Finley.

The axolotl lifted his head and chirped around a mouthful of fish.

I put my hands on my hips. "Don't you two gang up on me."

"You're never this chatty at night, Bree. What's got you all hot and bothered?" My sister's eyes narrowed in amused suspicion. "Or should I say *who*?"

I wished my nervous energy was because of Dominic. With Finley taken care of, I opened one of my pseudo-dresser drawers and dug out a clean pair of shorts and a sports bra. "I'm just nervous about the fight."

After a quick pout, Marissa dropped her gaze back to her phone. "Just keep your eye on the prize, Ree. Then Frankie will be free of this asinine debt and the Satos for good."

I loved my sister dearly, but I couldn't help my laugh. She was obsessed with impressing people, and adding new words to her vocabulary like asinine was just her newest endeavor to achieve that goal.

Wait…

I froze, my shirt halfway over my head. "What?"

A frown creased her forehead as she tapped away at the screen. "What what?"

"What do you mean about being free of the Satos?"

She gave a one-shoulder shrug. "Once she pays back the debt she owes them."

My mind stuttered to a stop. The words were said so casually, so unaware that my world had just imploded. "How do you know she owes the Satos?"

She paused her tapping long enough to glance at me like I was an idiot. "Because Frankie told me. Duh."

"When?"

"I don't know, dude, a few days ago," she said with an exaggerated huff. "She didn't tell you?"

"No." My voice was shaky, my breaths growing ragged.

Why hadn't Frankie told me?

Why hadn't Nic, for that matter?

Apparently, everyone knew except me.

"She probably didn't want to make things awkward between you and lover boy," Marissa said with a song-song note at the end, engrossed in her phone once again.

Clenching my jaw tight, I finished changing and headed for the gym.

Had I been a complete fool?

If Dominic knew about this debt, then there was only one logical reason he kept his involvement from me. He was Ichiro's heir, after all—heir and *spy*.

He was there to make sure the debt was paid. Or maybe he was tasked with interfering with and sabotaging our plans so we couldn't pay it back, which would explain the date of the fight moving up after implementing our ingenious massage idea. Subliminal was bound to be a true moneymaker managed by someone like Ichiro.

Now I really needed to channel my nervous energy, only this time it was fueled by a growing rage.

I mean, sure, I had secrets too, but nothing that affected Dominic the way this debt affected me and my life. My sister's life, too, and Frankie's! All the people I cared about most.

Maybe he assumed I already knew or that it didn't concern me somehow. I almost laughed.

Had he really lied to me this whole time? Used me?

If so, how had I not seen it before?

Or was there nothing to see?

Chewing on my lip hard enough to draw blood, I burst through the gym's front door and spun right back around. The next door over led up to Frankie's apartment complex, and someone had busted the lock years ago. I hauled the door open and stomped up the stairs, mulling the situation over.

In the very unlikely scenario that he didn't know about the debt and was truly innocent, then I couldn't involve him. His pride would have him trying to do something stupid like pay off the debt.

Sounded great on paper, but after everything I'd read about their family and learned from Dominic himself, going against Ichiro for my sake was sure to be a death sentence. Possibly for all of us.

There was a reason Ichiro Sato wanted this gym, and nothing would get in his way.

Whatever the case, I needed answers, and Frankie better be ready to face the hurricane headed her way—

Me.

Bree

As much as I wanted to shove Frankie's apartment door open so hard it slammed against the wall, I couldn't bring myself to do it. That much noise would bother our innocent neighbors. I settled for stomping in and closing the door harder than normal.

Wearing a fluffy pink robe, Frankie lounged on her worn, flower-patterned couch, watching a reality TV show and munching on popcorn. The bowl in her lap was so big, it almost needed a seat of its own.

Behind her, a narrow doorway led into the tiny galley kitchen while a door next to the TV opened into her bedroom and bathroom. Even combined, they weren't much bigger than the kitchen.

Without taking her eyes off the screen where some college-aged kids were working on a yacht, she patted the seat next to her. "Hey, kiddo. You hungry?"

I stood between her and the TV. "Why didn't you tell me?"

"Tell you what?" She tried to peer around me.

I sidestepped and blocked her view again. "About the Satos."

Squinting up at me, she flicked her hand toward the TV, pausing the show. "Is this a new guessin' game? What about the Satos?"

I crossed my arms. "That they're who you're in debt with."

Unfazed, she tossed another handful of popcorn in her mouth. "Not a big deal."

"How is it not a big deal?" I was so angry I could just throttle the woman. "You're the one who practically forced me onto that date with Dominic."

"How d'you figure I forced you?" Her eyebrows raised in an amused expression, turning the dial on my rage-o-meter from medium to high.

"It was your harebrained idea for us to fight, and then you locked me out of the gym when his limo showed up."

She tossed a piece of popcorn in the air and caught it in her mouth. "Oh, right. That was pretty dang funny."

"How could you keep this from me, Frankie?"

"Because of what you're doin' right now."

"Yeah? What's that?"

"Havin' a temper tantrum."

Oh, she did *not* just liken me to a toddler. If anyone behaved that way, it was Marissa. But two could play at that game. "Since it's apparently beyond your ability to understand, let me lay it out for you in simple terms."

She grinned. "Ooh. She's gettin' feisty. Go on then. I'm all ears."

"Dominic Sato never wanted to date me. He's the presumed heir to the Sato empire and has a vested interest in anything financial. If we owe him money, he's going to want to make sure it gets paid, no matter how low he has to sink."

Her look of shock was downright comical, but then she shook her head and laughed. "Sometimes you can be so obtuse, kiddo."

I was going to explode any moment now. "How exactly do you come to that conclusion?"

"Well, first of all, if the Satos wanted to make sure they got paid, they wouldn't hide it behind sneakery and fake datin'." She patted the seat next to her again.

My anger dissipated like a popped bubble. She might have been right about the Satos, but I wasn't being obtuse. I'd already considered what she said, which meant Dominic might not know about the debt after all.

But from her tone, I knew I was missing something. Story of my life. "They would if they wanted us to fail. Owning the gym would make them so much money."

She looked at me like I was a lost guppy. "Oh, hun. Don't you get it?"

"Obviously not." I plopped onto the couch beside her.

"That dimwitted Red Dragon was doomed the moment he laid eyes on you." She held the popcorn bowl out toward me, and I grabbed a handful.

"I still don't get it," I said before taking a bite.

As usual, Frankie had made the best stovetop popcorn. She poured melted butter over it so each kernel was drenched, then topped it off with a sprinkling of sea salt.

She pointed toward the TV, which was still paused. "What d'you see?"

On the screen, a young man and woman were frozen mid-grin while shaking hands on the deck of a boat. I knew from previous late-night binge sessions with her that these kids worked and lived on a luxury super yacht during charter season.

It was brainless entertainment. "I see your favorite show."

Frankie snorted, then started coughing. Leaning forward, she banged on her chest until it cleared. "Damn 'corn went down the wrong pipe. Look closer at the guy and how he's lookin' at her."

Lars, the guy in question, smiled at Samantha, who had just arrived as a new crew member. On the surface, it looked like he was simply happy to meet a new crew member. But his eyes...

Oh.

Oh.

He was head over heels. Love at first sight. Smitten as a kitten.

"That's not what—"

"It sure is, kiddo." Frankie chuckled and unpaused the show with a flick of her wrist. "Doomed, I tell you."

The show continued and cut to a brief clip of the guy in the interview room, pretending that he was struck by Cupid's arrow.

Munching on popcorn, I considered the implications of what Frankie was suggesting. If she was right, then Dominic wasn't playing me. He genuinely wanted to date me.

Evidence supported that theory, what with the insane amount of tulips decorating the gym and basement, plus all the time spent getting to know me via text and phone calls. That was quite the investment just to convince some poor girl she was special enough to win the attention of a Sato.

I knew all this to be true, but I wasn't convinced.

Well, that wasn't true. I *was* convinced his desire to date me was real. But I wasn't convinced he didn't know about his family's involvement in the debt. He was Ichiro's right-hand man, the most likely to take over the entire empire.

So if he did know, then I was confused about why he hadn't told me about owning the debt, at the very least. I was also angry he hadn't paid it or forgiven it, knowing that the gym was home to my sister and me.

If he truly cared about me, he would have done or said *something*.

But he didn't.

His family didn't need this paltry amount any more than I needed a new book.

Wait. Scratch that. I always needed new books. Books were one of the very few pleasures I had in life.

Okay, they didn't need our money any more than Marissa needed more clothes. Stuffed to bursting, her plastic dresser drawers hadn't closed all the way in years.

The Satos already had wealth and fame in spades. What more could they possibly gain by holding this over our heads?

Whatever the reason, I couldn't waste my time figuring it out until after Friday's fight. I wouldn't let my emotions interfere, which meant no more Dominic. And just in case my first theory was correct and Nic was playing me for a fool, I would keep my involvement in the fight a secret.

Grabbing another handful of popcorn, I focused on the show and did my best to ignore the uneasy feeling settling around my shoulders.

CHAPTER 24

Dominic

The sun crept over the horizon, casting a soft glow across Dominic's weary face. He stared at his reflection in the antique mirror hanging in the hallway of his grandfather's estate. Dark circles enveloped his bloodshot eyes, and the lines of exhaustion etched on his brow mocked him like thin scars left by an invisible enemy.

Gods, he looked like hell. It'd been another sleepless night. Another night spent reminding people to pay what they owed or face the consequences. This was what happened when one was tangled up in mobster shit.

His family's legacy pressed down on Dominic's shoulders like he carried the weight of the world. At this rate, his death would come far too quickly.

To make matters worse, he hadn't been able to see Bree again. Not since the motorcycle ride, and there was only so much satisfaction he could get from his hand and sexy messages or pictures of her.

He wanted the real thing, craved her scent and taste nearly

to obsession. He dreamed about how good she would taste coming against his mouth and woke with an aching need to be deep inside her.

Worse still, she'd hardly messaged him over the last two days and hadn't answered his calls. She claimed she was simply exhausted from prepping Subliminal for the upcoming fight that night, which made sense. It would be a full house.

Except something about her messages hadn't sat right with him and triggered a concern for her safety. He wouldn't put it past Ichiro to ruin something good in his bastard grandson's life, so he'd asked Rin to keep a close eye on her.

So far, everything was as it should be. She was working longer than normal hours, exactly as she'd said.

And yet.

Perhaps she'd finally realized just how much of a monster he could be and did the smart thing—run.

He ran a hand through his hair and sighed. This world of luxury and power came at too high a cost sometimes. Enough was enough. He had to put an end to the pyrocrystal dealings. That godsforsaken drug had taken over his life.

Giving his reflection one last weary glance, Dominic adjusted his collar and strode down the hallway.

He would claim what was rightfully his or die trying.

The familiar scent of sandalwood and corruption accosted him as he entered the study. Ichiro sat behind the massive oak desk, his gnarled fingers moving across some papers as he studied them.

Dominic cleared his throat. "We need to talk."

Ichiro looked up from his work, his dark eyes glinting dangerously behind his wire-rimmed spectacles. "Do we now?"

There was no sense in skirting around the issue. It was time to rip off the band-aid. "You need to name me as heir. Officially."

For a moment, the room seemed to grow darker, the tension between the two men palpable.

"Is that so?" the old man asked quietly.

Dominic hated these games with a passion so thick he could taste it. His grandfather wasn't looking for a response, and the silence stretched on as the weight of the demand sank deep into the air.

"You think you're better suited than the others?" Ichiro finally asked, leaning back in his chair and steepling his fingers.

"What others?" Dominic asked with a scornful laugh. "You know as well as anyone that no one else can follow in your footsteps."

The smile that tugged at the corners of his grandfather's lips sent a chill down his spine. It was the sort of grin that made Dominic feel like a human being toyed with by a particularly sadistic dragon.

"Very well," Ichiro said slowly, his voice low and lethal. "But remember, boy, there are consequences for failing your family. Are you prepared to face them?"

"You've made it very clear from the day I was born that I wasn't a welcome part of this family." Dominic's own voice was laced with a mixture of defiance and fury. "But I don't need to be welcome to be right, and I won't fail. Set your terms."

Breaking through the Sato family's dark legacy wouldn't be easy, but for Bree's safety, he was willing to do whatever it took.

The sunlight caught the glimmer of cruel mischief in Ichiro's eyes. "One last fight, and I will grant your wish."

Dominic stiffened. Outside of training with his friends and his bet with Bree, it had been years since he'd fought in the ring. He'd left that world behind.

Or so he'd thought.

"Why now?" he asked.

"Consider it payment for destroying my property."

Along with the shipping container filled with pyrocrystals, the entire warehouse had burned to the ground, just as Dominic had ordered. He'd been paying for it every day since. Hence, the dark circles beneath his eyes.

He smiled. "When do I fight?"

Ichiro tapped one of the papers sprawled across his desk. "You've likely heard that Ms. Delgado has announced a fight for this evening. She claims no one can beat this new mystery fighter. I want you to prove that fae woman wrong." His eyes flashed dangerously with red. "Prove that no one is stronger than a Sato dragon."

During his fighting years, Dominic had never lost a single match. He was the undeniable best—back then. But as everything does, he was getting older, and his last fight had almost killed him. The close call was his whole reason for getting out while he still could.

The difference now was Bree and keeping her safe from people like his grandfather, which meant he needed to speed up his plan's timeline.

Dominic nodded. "Fine. But when I win, you will announce me as your official heir. Tonight."

His grandfather's eyes narrowed in calculation, as if weighing the potential consequences of granting his full request. The air in the study grew thick and heavy, like a storm brewing on the horizon.

"Very well. But remember Dominic, your mother found out the hard way that forcing my hand comes with a steep price."

Ichiro's words were deliberate and cruel, designed to make him falter. But he had always been an outsider, standing on the fringes of this twisted family. And he'd be damned if he folded now.

No matter what price he had to pay, he would face it head-on. "I'll burn down every last corner of that gym if that's what it takes to win."

With a savage smile, the old man pushed back his chair and stood before offering his hand.

Dominic stepped forward, clasping his grandfather's forearm to seal the deal.

As Ichiro gripped his arm tight, his cold gaze seared through him. "There will be no turning back, boy. If you lose, you die."

Although he'd assumed that would be the case, hearing his death sentence spoken out loud chilled Dominic to the bone. "Good thing I never turn back."

Ichiro gave a curt nod. "As you say, let it be bound."

Wisps of red smoke curled around their enjoined arms. The vapor seeped into their skin, binding them with magic before disappearing.

It was done.

Leaving the suffocating confines of his grandfather's study, Dominic strode down the hall, each step echoing on the polished wood floor. The farther away he got, the more the weight lifted from his shoulders and soul.

He couldn't shake the feeling that he was stepping into the unknown, but whatever awaited him after the fight, he knew he wouldn't face it alone. The image of Bree's smiling face filled his heart, her presence a beacon of hope in the ever-present darkness.

With her in his life and by his side, there was nothing he couldn't overcome.

CHAPTER 25

Bree

Dressed and ready for the big fight, I paced restlessly in my room, stealing glances at the door that led into the main gym. As ready as I would ever be, anyway.

Every few minutes, I worked up the courage to peek out. Beneath the harsh spotlight, the boxing ring cast long shadows across the gym, and the crowd had tripled in size compared to the last fight, larger than any I'd seen here before.

True to her word, Frankie had brought in some big names from past years, including the Savage Wolf and the Wicked Witch. They both wore masks to protect their identities, but with their reputations, no one would dare mess with them anyway. Their mere presence was a huge draw for our members.

Excited murmurs drifted through the cracked door and fueled the anxiety churning in my gut:

"Have you heard anything about the mystery fighter?"

"No, but I've heard their opponent is one of Subliminal's best."

"Who is it?"

"Frankie's keeping it under wraps, but I'd pay a fortune to see the dragon back in action."

Smirking, I closed the door and resumed pacing. There was only one dragon they'd be referring to, and he'd retired years ago.

But as the conversations continued, the air around me crackled with anticipation. There was still time to change my mind...

Right?

My gaze flicked between the door and the floor, cold dread pooling deeper into my veins. This was such a terrible idea.

Not bothering to look up from her phone, Marissa sighed. She was sprawled across her rickety cot, her legs dangled over the side. "Will you relax? You're making me nervous."

"*You're* nervous?" I snapped. "Do you understand the consequences if I lose?"

"You'll win. You've trained all week and for years before that."

Trust Marissa to remain unfazed about such a monumental moment. She'd waltzed through earthquakes without blinking an eye.

"So have all the other fighters, but they don't have to worry about losing their homes."

Actually, I had no idea if that was true. Some of them weren't much better off than we were. Hopping on board that train of thought, my mind crept closer to chickening out.

Groaning, Marissa sat up and finally put her phone down. More like slammed it down on the bed with a dramatic flair. "Oh my god, stop. You've got this. Just do what you always do and show them who's boss just like you boss me around."

"Yeah, but you don't listen to me," I pointed out.

"Because I'm your sister, duh." She rolled her eyes. "It's my job not to listen. Doesn't mean you're not good at it."

"Aww. That may be the nicest thing you've ever said to me."

She shot me an annoyed look. "Don't get used to it."

Deep down, I knew she was right. I couldn't let my fears get the better of me. Not tonight. Too much was on the line. I had to keep my eye on the prize—our home. I couldn't worry about anyone else's situation right now.

I took a deep breath and tried to focus on something else. More like some*one* else, except that line of thinking didn't get far.

The door opened, allowing a torrent of excited babble to flood in.

I glanced over at Finley's aquarium, relieved to see the towel I'd draped over it was still in place. With the gym packed with so many unfamiliar faces, the last thing we needed was someone wandering in and catching sight of the little guy, or worse.

Frankie came in and shut the door before giving me a look over the railing that raised the hairs along my arms. Bad news was incoming.

She met me at the base of the steps. "Uh, so, I've got news."

"I figured as much."

Marissa was by my side in a flash. "Good or bad?"

"Does it matter?" I just needed to know what was causing that look on Frankie's face.

"It might if—"

"It's the Red Dragon," Frankie cut in, knowing from experience how long my sister and I could go back and forth.

"What about him?" I asked, my heart in my throat.

Ignoring him over the past two days had been harder than I

thought. I'd planned on ignoring him completely, only to find myself returning a few texts here and there. Being a people pleaser royally sucked sometimes.

I wasn't ready to talk about the debt until after this fight, but I also didn't want him showing up unexpectedly and forcing the conversation. Keeping my mouth shut wouldn't be an option if I saw him in person right now because I was still furious, but also because I hated having this rift between us.

And he didn't even know there was a rift.

Had something happened to him before I had the chance to confront him?

Frankie held up her phone, displaying a chain of text messages from Ichiro Sato about Dominic. "He's your opponent tonight."

As Marissa snatched the phone to read the conversation, the world around me started to spin. My lungs burned and my vision blurred, and for a moment, I was afraid that I was going to pass out.

This couldn't be happening.

Nausea churned in my gut. I rested a hand over my stomach. "I think I might be sick."

Frankie grabbed our small trash can and held it up. "I'm sorry, kiddo. I told him I already had someone. I tried."

"Goddess below, is Ichiro always that arrogant?" Marissa handed the phone back to Frankie with a look of disgust.

"Yes."

Clutching the trash can to my chest like an anchor, I met Frankie's gaze. "Why is he fighting?"

"I don't know." Violet flashed through her irises. "All I know is the old dragon won't take no for an answer. If it wasn't for this godsdamned debt..."

She didn't need to finish the sentence. We all knew that Frankie wasn't one to be pushed around, but with the gym and our homes at stake, Sato had her backed into a corner.

"Then I won't fight." I sat on the edge of my bed, setting the can between my legs. For the most part, the nausea had passed, but I didn't trust my body just yet. "Throw someone else in the ring. Anyone."

My boss's expression turned sympathetic, and I knew I was fighting a losing battle. "He'd know. You're the only unknown fighter I've got."

"Forget Grandpa Asshat." Marissa waved a hand dismissively. "You've fought Dominic before and won. Just do it again."

I wished I could laugh at the nickname, but the situation was so much worse than just fighting him. The Gifted forums and gossip websites could only provide so much information about the Sato family. There was more she, or anyone else, didn't know about Dominic and his family.

If he was fighting again after this many years, after his close call the last time he fought, something big was happening, or something terrible. Neither option would be good.

Leaning forward, I dropped my head into my hands. "The only reason I won last time is because I had the element of surprise. Now he knows exactly what I am. I won't be that lucky again."

"You think he's going to try to win against his girlfriend?"

"He has no choice."

My sister crossed her arms. "Why?"

Before I could explain, the door opened with a bang.

I jumped off the cot, fists raised. But then my mouth dropped open in surprise.

With the gym's spotlights illuminating the background, a familiar figure strode in and closed the door behind him. His whiskey-hued gaze met mine with a burning intensity that made me gulp.

Dominic.

CHAPTER 26

Bree

"Good evening ladies." Dominic's sensual voice wrapped around me, warming me from within. He wore a black t-shirt that clung to his muscles like a second skin and black athletic shorts, stitched with a red dragon on one leg—his fighting clothes. "Can Bree and I have a moment alone please?"

"I gotta head back out there anyway," Frankie said, casting me a final look that said it all.

There was no turning back.

Marissa leaned closer to me. "Want me to stay?"

I shook my head. I needed to face him on my own, no matter how difficult. But honestly, I had no idea what I was going to say or do. My thoughts and emotions were in complete chaos.

After they both left, Dominic met me in the middle of the room. His beautiful eyes roved over my face. "You've been avoiding me."

"Like I said in my messages, I've just been really busy." I dropped my focus to cracks on the floor, unable to lie while looking at him.

His fingers lifted my chin until I met his gaze again. "It's more than that. Talk to me."

I couldn't do this. I needed space. Taking a step back, I shook my head, not really sure what I was saying no to. "Why are you fighting?"

He studied me for a moment before answering. "I made a deal with Ichiro. If I agreed to this fight, he would publicly name me as his heir."

My stomach dropped into the deepest darkest ocean. "But only if you win, right?"

His lips pulled up into a delicious grin. Tides, I wanted to kiss those lips until I forgot about everything else.

"You know I always win, darlin'."

"Not always," I said quietly.

Linking his fingers between mine, he raised both my hands to his warm lips. "Are you worried about me getting hurt?"

That and so much more. I yanked my hands out of his. "I don't understand why you would even want to be his heir, Nic. Everything about that family is corrupt."

His expression hardened, but I knew from our previous talks his anger wasn't directed at me. "That's exactly why I need to do this. It's worse than you know. He's—" He stopped short as if contemplating whether to continue, then asked, "Do you know what pyrocrystals are?"

I shook my head.

"They're formed during a dragon's spirit bonding ceremony and help enhance the new connection," he explained. "Ichiro has figured out a way to create them en masse and is selling them to Gifted people."

I didn't quite understand what he was implying. "Why is that bad?"

The lines along his jaw moved as he clenched his teeth. "They're a drug to anyone not bonded to a dragon, a very powerful and addictive drug. He's using them to force submission and seize control. Soon, he'll be more unstoppable than he already is."

Oh, crab on a coconut. Ichiro was already one of the most powerful people in the city, if not the most. "So, you want to take over and put a stop to it, I'm guessing."

"I'm not a good man, Bree." His gaze darkened, but it only served to make him more attractive. "I've never pretended to be. But this goes too far. He's crossed a line, and the only one who stands a chance going against my grandfather is me."

My heart ached as cracks formed, ready to break apart completely. I didn't agree with him at all. He *was* a good man, but one stuck in an unfortunate situation, having to make difficult decisions. I could relate.

"Can't you fight him without having to be named heir?"

"The only way to put an end to this is from the inside. There are too many variables involved." He stepped closer and cupped my face in my hands. The cracks in my heart grew bigger. "I know this is difficult and that I'm asking a lot, but trust me. Please. I wouldn't do anything to hurt you, and I would kill anyone who tried to."

I closed my eyes and leaned against his palm, trying to find some comfort in his touch. Unfortunately, there was no comfort to be found.

The deep clang of a bell echoed across the gym, followed by erupting cheers that shook the walls.

That would be Frankie announcing the fight and hyping up the crowd. We only had a few more minutes, which meant I needed to make a decision—fast.

"What happens if you lose?" I whispered, my voice thick with emotion.

He shrugged and smiled, much too casually for his next words. "He'll kill me."

And just like that, my decision was made.

If he won, Marissa and I would lose our home. There was no way Ichiro would let us live in the basement rent-free, and I couldn't afford it on my current salary. I couldn't afford any place.

Marissa and I had been homeless and hungry before, we could do it again. And Frankie was scrappy enough to survive the apocalypse. We could come back from those things.

But if I won, Dominic would lose more than just the fight.

There was no coming back from death.

The illegal fights at Subliminal were brutal, partly to give the audience a good show, but also because Gifted people healed at faster-than-human rates. It took mass destruction to win, and in some cases, one or both opponents died from their injuries.

He needed to win, but there was no way he was going to fight me like that tonight. Despite his tough exterior and the arrogance he wore like a shield, Dominic wouldn't hurt the people he cared about, which meant he wouldn't hurt me, even to save his own life.

Unless...

...he hated me.

My heart hammered viciously against my ribs as an idea formed. The only true way I could get him to feel nothing but violent hatred toward me. It would be despicable, but it would work.

Could I do that to him?

To us?

The bell rang again, and I knew my time had run out. Frankie would expect us in just another minute. I had no other choice.

I swallowed the lump forming in my throat and squared my shoulders. Channeling Marissa's sass with an inner grimace, I twisted my lips into a smirk. "Ready for round two, lizard boy?"

Dominic's bewildered look would have been funny in any other situation. "Round two of what?"

I gestured toward the gym. "They're waiting for us to fight."

"You." His eyes widened, and his gaze traveled the length of my body, taking in my Subliminal shorts and sports bra. He finally seemed to comprehend my outfit. "You're the mystery opponent?"

I gazed at him coolly. "Do you have a problem with that?"

The crowd's cheers grew thunderous, but it was nothing compared to my pulse drumming in my ears.

He let out a short, surprised laugh. "I'm not fighting you."

"Scared you'll lose again, only this time in front of your adoring fans?"

"Scared of hurting you," he said softly, reaching for me. "I have to win this."

I backed away from him. I couldn't do this if he touched me. "So win."

"Aren't you worried about everyone else figuring out that it's you?" he asked. "Regulars will notice you're not watching the fight."

"Frankie has that covered."

My boss had created an illusion of me that would remain in her office, reading a book. No one would find that suspicious behavior for me, even for a big fight night. The illusion could handle simple replies that shut down conversations before they could happen.

Thank the tide for fae magic.

"Bree, you know how I feel about you." The pleading in his voice just about killed me. "Please back down."

The time had come to smash his hopes and drown his dreams.

"You know what I am, Nic." I grabbed my mask and headed for the steps that led to the gym. Resting my free hand on the railing, I raised my gaze to meet his surprised one. This was it, the kill shot. "Did it not occur to you that what you've seen and everything you feel are lies?"

His entire body tensed, and crimson light flared within his eyes. The Red Dragon had awakened. "Stop. I know what you're trying to do."

"Do you?" I smiled cruelly, hating myself for every second of this charade, this betrayal. "How well do you think you actually know me, Dominic?"

"Better than you think I do."

When I allowed someone to truly feel my magic rather than block them from sensing it, the experience was far from pleasant. A rather revolting sensation, or so I've been told. At least for landlubbers who weren't used to the slick, intimate caress of a sea creature like me.

I cast my magic out like a net, looping it around Dominic's mind, and encouraged him to kneel with a single lyrical note, "*Fa.*"

A startled grunt escaped his lips before he fell to his knees. His eyes opened wide.

My hands trembled, so I gripped the railing tighter and hoped he was too stunned to notice.

"That was just a taste, *darlin'*." I climbed the steps and grabbed the door handle. With my back to him, I squeezed my eyes shut, holding back the tears threatening to spill.

No, I wasn't just a sea creature...

...I was a monster.

CHAPTER 27

Dominic

Dominic stared at Bree's back. Her magic still pinned him down, gliding through his mind with a salty aftertaste. She was much more powerful than she let on, possibly more than even she knew.

One word, one simple musical note, had taken him to his knees.

But he was unwilling to accept her words as truth. It didn't make any sense. None of this did. "Why?"

With her hand on the door handle, she glanced over her shoulder. A look of venomous disdain marred her otherwise delicate features. "The Satos will own this gym over my dead body."

She slid her mask over her face, activating the magic that hid her identity, and entered the gym as an unidentifiable nobody. A roar of applause and excited shouting followed in her wake.

"And here she is, folks," Frankie's amplified voice resounded across the gym, "our mystery fighter, the likes of which you've never seen before. I present the Sultry Siren!"

It wasn't until the door clicked shut that Bree's magic withdrew and Dominic and his dragon could move again. He stood on unsteady legs, Jou roaring with fury and defiance within his mind.

Not once in his entire life had he felt as shaken as he did then.

What the fuck had just happened?

He'd come in to tell her about the deal with Ichiro and expected some pushback. What he hadn't expected was to have his entire world destroyed in a matter of moments.

Once again, he replayed the conversation in his mind. There was no way what Bree had said was true. He would know if he was being controlled by her magic that way.

Wouldn't he?

As he remembered her singing at the gym and the entranced sensation that had washed over him hearing her voice, he grew even more confused and uncertain. Jou's menacing rumbles mirrored his frustration. If she had used her ability to make him forget, he would never know.

And what had she meant about the Satos owning the gym?

As far as Dominic knew, after tonight, the Satos were finished with Subliminal. This was a one-and-done situation. Frankie was a force to be reckoned with, and Ichiro wasn't willing to go toe-to-toe with her.

Had the old man kept something from him?

If so, why?

Dread seeped into his bones, cold as ice. The only reason he could think of was if his grandfather knew about Dominic's plan. His *real* plan, the one he'd been hiding for years and the details of which only his closest friends knew.

Except, if Ichiro had somehow found out, then Dominic

would be dead already. The old man had no use for games like this.

Had he just made a huge mistake telling Bree about Ichiro and the pyrocrystals?

Would she use that knowledge against him?

The door opened and Frankie stuck her head in, scowling. "Get a move on, dragon. We're all waitin' for you."

That damned fae woman was gone before he could stop her. He clenched his fists in frustration.

There was only one person who could make sense of it all.

He strode up the steps and threw open the door. Immediately, the spotlight found him and followed his approach to the ring.

A hush washed over the gym. Wide-eyed fans stared on either side of him, hands reaching out to brush him reverently as he passed.

No one had fought without a mask before. While Dominic had initially intended to wear one, now, he wanted to make a statement. He was done hiding.

"Well, ladies and gents, this is a first," Frankie's voice boomed through the speakers. "I give you Dominic Sato, the undefeated Red Dragon and Subliminal champion!"

The audience went wild with thunderous applause as he stepped up onto the ring and ducked beneath the ropes. The only person he concerned himself with was facing him. Her facial features were as unknown to him as anyone else, but he had memorized every inch of her body. He would know her anywhere.

Like their last fight, Bree was soaked from head to foot. Beads of water dripped down her face and body and pooled on the mat beneath her bare feet. An empty bucket rested in the corner.

Ocean-blue eyes gazed back at him behind her mask, not an ounce of regret to be seen. "For a moment there, I thought you were too much of a coward to face me again."

While Frankie continued to address the crowd, building them up to even higher levels and encouraging bets, Dominic studied the woman he'd fallen for, his chosen mate. "I don't believe this was all a lie."

She smirked. "And people call me naïve."

Frankie climbed into the center of the ring and glanced at each of them. "You two ready?"

Without hesitation, Bree nodded.

He couldn't fight her, not like this. Something wasn't right. Their feelings for each other were real. You couldn't fake what they had, not even with magic.

But if he didn't fight and win, Ichiro would kill him. Or try to, at any rate.

Either way, he was fucked.

"Frankie, tell me what's going on," Dominic growled.

The fae woman looked him in the eye. "Whatever she told you, I'd believe it because ready or not, this is happenin'. Begin!" she cried out before ducking out of the ring.

Immediately, Bree raised her hands, drawing water from the pool at her feet. With a quick, fluid motion, she shaped the water into dozens of frozen shards and unleashed them. The water bullets flew toward him with deadly accuracy.

As the audience gasped and cheered on this new contender, Dominic dove to the side. One of the razor-sharp shards tore through his arm, bringing a hiss to his lips, and Jou writhed against the tight leash keeping him contained.

He would find out what was happening with Bree, but he couldn't if she killed him first. He unleashed his dragon.

The beast ripped away from his skin and darted toward Bree faster than a striking snake.

Except she was ready for him.

A torrent of water surged upward, knocking the dragon off course and dousing some of his flames. With a roar of fury, Jou spun to the side and circled over the crowd's head, stoking his fiery scales back to life.

Bree called the water to her, wrapping the torrent around her body until it clung like a second skin. Its shimmering embrace accentuated her lithe figure as she moved. The water danced with her like a suit of armor, rippling and flowing with an otherworldly grace.

Dominic stood mesmerized as the ever-shifting patterns of light played tricks on his eyes and the sound of tinkling water followed her steps. She was powerful and stunning, a goddess incarnate.

Water streamed down her arms and wrapped around her fists, which she raised in a boxing stance. "Let's dance, dragon."

He couldn't fight her, and it had nothing to do with their contrasting abilities. The fight would be difficult, and she could very well win again. Hell, she deserved to win.

But he couldn't fight her until he knew the truth. He dropped his fists, ignoring the angry jeers and boos directed at him.

Confusion swept through Bree's gaze. "You're giving up?"

"I have to know the truth."

She narrowed her eyes and took a step toward him. "I told you the truth."

"I don't believe it."

"Said every narcissistic man ever." Her scathing words cut deep to his core. "You guys never seem to believe a woman may not actually be into you. It's pathetic."

Rage flared to life in Dominic's chest, and Jou roared behind him, ready to strike. But he held up his hand to stop the beast. "Tell me why you're fighting."

"Because I enjoy bringing the mighty Red Dragon to his knees." She darted in, jabbing at his unprotected middle.

Instead of the softness one might expect from the water flowing over her fist, her punch felt like a battering ram that sent shockwaves through his body and might have broken a few ribs. He inhaled sharply as an intense and immediate chill spread.

A deluge of water rapidly engulfed him as if he'd been caught in a relentless downpour, but one that originated from a single, powerful point of impact. He gasped for breath and struggled to maintain his footing.

Whether from Ichiro's or Bree's hands, Dominic knew he would likely die that day.

CHAPTER 28

Bree

I let my watery attack subside, hoping the assault would be enough to force his hand. To make him *win*.

Dominic shook his head, flinging water everywhere, and swiped a hand down his face. "What did you mean about the gym? Why would my family own the gym?"

I drew my eyebrows together. Was it possible he wasn't involved or even aware? "Don't pretend like you don't know."

His face contorted with frustration. "Know what?"

If he truly wasn't involved, then I'd been angry for no reason. Worse, for two days, I'd avoided the man I lov—

I blinked. Crab on a hot plate. This had to end. I needed him to win before my resolve crumbled. I couldn't let him go against Ichiro over this debt, and I definitely couldn't let him die.

Taking a deep breath, I started to sing, "*But oh...*"

He staggered backward with wide eyes. Rumbling behind him, his dragon's red eyes fixed on me with deadly intensity.

Infusing each word with my magic, I continued the song

he'd walked in on me singing while mopping, *"...if we call the whole thing off..."*

He clutched at his chest as my magic took hold, tendrils of lyrical power curling around his heart and squeezing. As his face contorted with pain, his dragon reared back on two feet, its head rising several feet above Dominic's.

The crowd had gone silent, waiting with bated breath for what came next.

"Then we must part." Each word tightened my grip on his soul, and I moved toward him. *"And oh, if we ever part..."*

As he blinked and then narrowed his eyes, I knew the song had worked. My magic had made him believe I was the enemy, that I'd betrayed him. My heart withered inside my chest.

"...then that might break my heart."

With a thunderous roar, Dominic swung his fist at my chest. At the same time, his dragon launched itself toward me in a blaze of fury. Their double blow hit me with the force of a breaching whale.

My feet left the mat as I flew out of the ring. Landing hard on my back against the cement floor, pain exploded across my entire body. My vision blurred as the wind whooshed out of me, and I gasped for air.

Sometimes, it really stunk to do the right thing. And hurt. So much hurt. Ouch.

My head throbbed as the crowd cheered for the victorious Red Dragon, and I hauled myself up to sit with a grimace. Not that I'd expected anyone to rush over and help me, considering no one had a clue who I was with this mask on, but it would have been nice.

Instead, I was basically out of sight, out of mind.

A familiar figure pushed her way through and knelt beside

me. Marissa's blue eyes were wide with fear, and she leaned close to whisper, "We have to go. *Now.*"

Nothing had ever scared me so much in my entire life than the look on her face. Ice practically formed in my veins, the fight forgotten. I tried to stand, but she held me down with a tight grip on my arm.

She nodded in the direction of the basement door, hidden behind a sea of legs. Before I had a chance to ask her what had happened, she dove between limbs while staying crouched down.

Wincing as my battered body protested each movement, I followed after her. Everything would heal soon, but not fast enough. Just before I ducked inside the open door, I glanced back at the ring.

Dominic leaned against the ropes, his chest heaving. Beneath furrowed brows, he scanned the audience until his gaze locked on mine. Anger, hurt, and confusion filled his expression, breaking my heart all over again.

I urged every ounce of my heart and soul into my gaze and smiled. My magic would last for a few days, and I wanted him to know how I truly felt when he looked back on this moment.

The crowd shifted, hiding him from view.

When we were safely inside our room and the door locked, Marissa whirled to face me. "They found us."

Oh, thank the tides. I slumped back against the door. "I know."

"What do you mean, 'you know'? Why aren't you freaking out like I am?" She ran down the steps and grabbed a bag from under her bed. Throwing it on the bed, she rummaged through her drawers.

"You don't need to pack just yet." I pushed off the door and descended the stairs, each step heavy with exhaustion. "I saw Demetri two days ago. But he said he wasn't here to bring us home. "

Marissa shook her head, her face paler than ever as she stuffed clothes into her bag. "No, not Demetri. I saw Sidon. We have to leave."

Oh...

Fuck.

Sidon was King Ateleíotes's right-hand man and royal assassin. Ateleíotes, as in our father's worst enemy and father to my betrothed. There was only one reason why the hunter would be here, not just on land but in Subliminal.

"Where did you see him?" My voice shook as I removed the towel covering Finley's tank.

The little axolotl blinked sleepy eyes against the sudden light. While he much preferred staying in water all day every day, his kind could survive without it for a few days. One small blessing on a night like tonight.

"Out there." She gestured toward the gym door before rushing past me into the bathroom. A moment later, she came back out with most of her toiletries gathered in her arms. "He was watching the fight and based on his expression, he knows it was you." She shoved her toiletries into the bag with her clothes. "Or maybe he thought it was me. Whatever. It doesn't matter. We gotta go."

The blood drained from my face. Things were moving too quickly for me to process properly. I had just betrayed the man I had tumbled head over tail for to save his life, only to find out mine might be in jeopardy. Mine *and* Marissa's.

I knew someone had been following me, but when I saw Demetrius, I stopped worrying. I had been so wrapped up in my own drama, I'd failed at my one purpose in life—keeping my sister safe.

How stupid and selfish could I be?

Apparently, very.

My sister's face popped up in front of mine. "Move, damnit!"

And so I did.

Dominic

Dominic leaned against the ropes of the ring, his chest heaving as he struggled to catch his breath. His knuckles stung and his muscles screamed in protest, but a surge of adrenaline still coursed through his veins, dulling the pain.

He wasn't even sure what had just happened. One moment he was waiting for Bree to knock him out and claim the win, and the next he hated her with every fiber of his being for bewitching and deceiving him.

His world had flipped upside down with her song, and he and Jou had reacted on instinct. His conflicting emotions continued to wage war within him even as his fans went wild and his dragon disappeared beneath his skin.

"The Red Dragon is victorious once again!" Frankie's voice boomed through the arena, nearly drowned out by the chants.

The accolades washed over him in a dull roar as his gaze searched the faces for Bree. There—her hunched figure paused at the back of the gym and turned to meet his gaze. A bittersweet smile graced her lips before the throng swallowed her whole.

Why was she leaving without a word?

And why did she look so damn pleased that he'd won?

He clenched his fists, his knuckles turning white. He wanted to chase after her, drag the truth from her lips once and for all, but the crowd hemmed him in, their jubilant celebration trapping him in place.

Gritting his teeth, he forced a smile and raised his hands in acknowledgment, soaking in their adulation. But beneath the clamor, beneath the triumph, his thoughts were consumed by the siren. She'd seemed so genuine, weaving herself into his life until he couldn't imagine a day without her.

How could she do this to him? Deceive him like this?

Anger and something else—something far more dangerous —rose in his chest, mingling with the confusion and heartache.

Betrayal.

The cheers became a deafening soundtrack, helping to drown out the pain in his heart. He refused to let his turbulent emotions overtake him, refused to give into the darkness that whispered at the edges of his mind.

Tonight, he'd celebrate, but after that?

After that, he would demand answers. He needed to know if she would tell Ichiro or anyone else his plans for shutting down the pyrocrystal trafficking.

He would drag the answers from her traitorous mouth by any means necessary.

A FEW DAYS LATER, DOMINIC SAT IN HIS OFFICE WITH Aaron, sorting through stacks of paperwork to finalize his future ownership of the Sato's business dealings. The room echoed with the sounds of shuffling papers and clicking pens as the accountant ensured Dominic signed every page.

Since they bound their deal with magic, Ichiro had announced Dominic as the official heir shortly after the fight. No one had been surprised, but not even Kenzo's bitter expression could lift Dominic's spirits.

In the days following the fight, his focus kept drifting to the unanswered questions plaguing his thoughts. No matter how hard he tried to focus on the tasks at hand, his mind kept circling back to that last moment he'd seen Bree.

Her gentle smile haunted him.

When the last signature was inked and the final account updated, relief washed over Dominic in a cool wave. The crushing weight of secrecy he'd carried for years slowly lifted from his shoulders.

But beneath the relief lingered a numbness he couldn't shake. His thoughts drifted to Bree's departure, the way she'd slipped from his life without a trace. Day by day, his hatred for her lessened until he wondered why the feeling had been so strong.

Aaron clipped the stack of papers together before clapping him on the back with a grin. "Congratulations. Drinks are on me tonight."

He forced a smile and nodded. "Sounds good."

As much as he wanted to celebrate their victory and launch into the next phase of their plan, he couldn't. Not fully.

The beautiful siren had turned his carefully ordered world upside down, then ghosted him. He ran a hand through his hair, frustration gnawing at his composure. Now that his takeover was official, he needed to understand why she'd deceived him.

Betrayal or not, he wasn't sure he could let her go.

The office door creaked open, stirring Dominic from his thoughts. Frankie stood in the doorway, a key ring clutched in her hand. A deep crease lined her forehead as she walked toward his desk.

Aaron shot him a glance, asking without words whether he should leave.

Dominic shook his head and sighed. He was too mentally exhausted to deal with the fae woman alone. "What do you need, Frankie?"

"Just droppin' off the keys." She tossed the jangling bundle onto his desk. "These belong to the gym, which now belongs to the Sato family. Congrats. Again."

His brows furrowed in confusion as he picked up the keys, studying them. "How did that happen?"

"Your grandfather and I had a little bit of a debt situation goin' on," Frankie explained, a hint of anger tinting her gruff voice. "It was s'posed to be temporary, but Ichiro sped up the timeline. We didn't raise enough money in time, so it's yours now."

The memory hit him like a punch in the gut—Bree had said he would own the gym over her dead body. His mind raced, trying to connect the dots. "Is this why Bree agreed to fight?"

"You betcha. She was hopin' to settle the debt with her win." She studied his face and grimaced. "I, uh, didn't realize you didn't know. I thought she told you right before you two fought."

"She was trying to save the gym?"

"Well, that and her home, you big dummy. Her entire livelihood."

Everything Bree had done suddenly took on a new meaning.

She had deceived him, yes, but not in the way he thought. She had sacrificed her home for *him*.

Dominic's chest tightened with a mix of frustration and concern, but mostly, a burning desire to find Bree and make things right. He needed to know the whole truth, to understand why she had kept him in the dark. Had he known, he could have helped her.

His chair scraped against the floor as he stood abruptly. "Is she at Subliminal?"

"Hold your dragon, cowboy. She left a note." Frankie's voice was heavy with regret. "Says she's sorry for deceivin' us both. I haven't seen her or Marissa since that night."

Dominic's mouth went dry. Why, after everything they'd gone through, did she think running away was the right choice?

The gym keys grew heavy in his hand, serving as a reminder of the path he needed to take. His plans could wait.

He wouldn't rest until he found her.

THE END

Find out what happens next when Bree must return to the sea in **SIREN'S GIFT**, book 2 of **WILD MAGIC: SIREN'S SECRET!**

Join my Facebook reader group — **MIRRO'S MAGICAL MORTALS** — to discuss *Siren's Blood* with fellow fans!

CONVERSATION STARTERS:

- Where will Bree and Marissa go next?

- How do you think Bree's mother died, and do you think it was really Bree's fault?
- What does Dominic plan to do with Ichiro?
- Based on Demetrius's visit, what trouble might be brewing back in the sea kingdom?
- Will Kenzo make it out of book 2 alive?

Love the nerdy heroine type? Then you have to meet Serafina from my **IMMORTAL RELICS** series, where Roman mythology and wry humor blend with magic, mayhem, and monsters. The series is available at major retailers in ebook and print!

Have a fondness for morally grey characters? Then don't miss **THE LAST PHOENIX** series, where a bloodsucking client, a sexier-than-sin agent, and a murder just made life a whole lot deadlier for Veronica Neill.

Wherever you go from here, happy reading!

Acknowledgments

As with all my books, I couldn't have done this without the support of my family, friends, and fans. Thank you for coming on this journey with me.

A special thank you to all the Kickstarter backers who brought this book to life. The Siren's Call backers went above and beyond—Tori Jade Bulmer, Shiboune Thill, Aaron, Valerie Galderisi, and Sherry Mock.

A big thank you to Tricia Beninato of Burning Phoenix Covers for the gorgeous ebook and paperback cover design!

I couldn't have done this without the help and support of the FAKA group (IYKYK). Seriously, you guys refilled my creative well at just the right time. Thank you.

Getting my books visible on platforms like Kickstarter and big retailers and into readers' hands is not easy, but my readers and fans keep me going when it sometimes feels too tough to continue.

If you want to keep a your favorite author writing and publishing, buy their books and share them with friends.

Onward and upward!

About the Author

Stephanie Mirro is an Amazon Charts bestselling author and best known for ***The Last Phoenix*** urban fantasy romance series. Stephanie's lifetime love of ancient mythology led to a college major in the Classics, which wasn't as much fun as writing her own fantastical mythology stories. But that education, combined with an overactive imagination and a love for all things fantasy, resulted in a writing career.

Although born and raised in the Southern Arizona desert, Stephanie now resides in Georgia with her husband, two kids, and two furbabies. This thing called "seasons" is still magical.

Interested in the longer, more entertaining story? Visit stephaniemirro.com/about

www.ingramcontent.com/pod-product-compliance
Lightning Source LLC
Chambersburg PA
CBHW020753190726
48285CB00006B/2015